DR. YEN SIN:
THE MYSTERY OF THE SINGING MUMMIES

THE INVISIBLE PERIL
DR. YEN SIN™

THE MYSTERY OF
THE SINGING MUMMIES

By Donald E. Keyhoe

ALTUS PRESS • 2017

EDITED AND DESIGNED BY

Matthew Moring

PUBLISHING HISTORY

"The Mystery of the Singing Mummies" originally appeared in the September/October, 1936 (Vol. 1, No. 3) issue of *Dr. Yen Sin* magazine. Copyright 1936 by Popular Publications, Inc. Copyright renewed 1963 and assigned to Steeger Properties, LLC. All rights reserved.

CHAPTER 1
THE LIVING DEAD

THE DISGUISE was almost perfect. The wrinkled nut vender squatted beside his cart, seemed just another aged Chinese, drowsing over his pipe.

With a gloomy night and fog from the Golden Gate half-shrouding Chinatown's hills, there appeared little chance for detection.

But he knew he was being watched.

Sleepily, he raised his left hand to his long clay pipe. Cupped in his yellowed fingers was a tiny mirror. He held it back of the bowl, turning it slowly to right and left. The bazaars behind him were dark. He tilted the glass up toward the curling, pagoda roofs, then down toward a narrow passage which ran between two buildings. No one was visible, but the blackness of the passage was impenetrable.

Somewhere off in the fog-shadowed city a clock struck the half-hour to midnight. A moment later, a taxicab swung around the corner from Grant Avenue. The nut vender watched through made-up, slitted eyes. The engine began to miss as the cab started up the slope. With a sputter, the machine edged in to the curb, fifty feet away.

The driver, a ruddy-faced youth with his cap drawn over his eyes, climbed out and lifted the hood. He tested the spark-plugs,

1

Eric fired at the glowing circle in the window which had become the face of Doctor Yen Sin.

began to tap at the carburetor. The wrinkled nut vender listened, carefully counting the taps.

A shuffling coolie paused to watch the driver. The nut vender stealthily reached out toward the cane which lay at his side. But the coolie went on. As the driver tinkered with his engine, a thin stream of humanity passed by—a group of American

tourists, returning to their hotel; an old Chinese woman in black trousers and coat, her clogs clicking on the sidewalk; two almond-eyed girls and their escorts, all smartly dressed in American style; and a stolid Chinese with a pigtail.

Seemingly drowsing over his pipe, the nut vendor watched and listened. There was nothing suspicious, and yet—

His right hand moved again toward the cane, for a furtive sound had come from the passage behind him. A soft, frightened voice instantly spoke, in the language of old Cathay.

"Make no sign, Sleepless One—it is a friend!"

The vender shifted his mirror, and a face of exotic loveliness showed vaguely from the shadows. The girl came a step closer, and he caught the haunting fragrance of some rare Oriental perfume.

"Can you hear me?" her red lips whispered.

"I am listening," he mumbled, without removing his pipe. "But I hear one I cannot always trust."

"You must believe me tonight!" she said desperately. "You and Eric Gordon are in danger. They suspect you already, and when they find him—"

"Where is the Invisible Emperor?" the man asked in a low voice.

The girl shrank back. "I can't tell you," she moaned. "You know what it would mean if—"

She broke off with a stifled cry, and the vender saw she was staring at the taxi driver.

"It's Eric!" she gasped. "Now they will be sure! You should never have let him do this!"

"He has been searching for you," the man returned grimly. "He hopes to rescue you from Doctor Yen Sin."

"No, he must forget me!" she said wildly. "Go quickly, both of you! If you value your lives, be far from Chinatown by midnight!"

In her frantic warning, she had taken a step forward. The man by the cart went rigid. Mirrored in the glass was the face of a yellow assassin just behind the girl!

TWO SAFFRON hands were reaching out to clutch her by the throat. The vender jumped to his feet, snatching up his cane. With a squeal of rage, the Chinese leaped back. One hand darted under his coat and reappeared with a gun.

But the vender's hand was quicker. Steel flashed, and a slender blade hissed from the sword cane. The assassin, pistol half drawn, tried to spring back of the girl. The vender lunged with the skill of a practiced fencer. A gurgling cry, the crash of a wild-aimed shot, and the Chinese sank to the ground.

The taxi driver had started to run toward the spot, but there came a sudden thudding of feet from the gloom. He whirled, gave a shout.

"Come on, Michael! They're trying to gang us!"

The taller man freed his dripping sword and spun around. The girl had crouched back in the shadows, unseen by the taxi driver.

"Run!" the vender told her swiftly.

He dashed for the cab as she vanished into the passage. Something whizzed close to him and scraped along the sidewalk. The driver fired at the Chinese who had thrown the knife, and the killer crumpled without a sound.

"Take the wheel, Eric!" clipped the disguised vender. He leaped sidewise, thrust viciously at an Oriental who sprang from behind the car. The man tottered back, pierced squarely through the heart.

Eric Gordon hurdled the man he had shot, and jumped into the taxi. Two more assassins dashed from the shadowy doorway of the nearest bazaar. The man with the sword sprang to the running-board. As the car lurched ahead, he tossed the weapon inside and scooped up Eric's pistol. The scarred face of a Chinese gunman showed near a misty street light. Two shots thundered almost as one. The Chinese screamed and sprawled to the walk.

The pseu-do-vender jumped into the rear of the cab, and Eric sent it careening around a corner. A last burst of shots died out.

"Phew!" said Eric fervently. "I thought it was curtains that time."

"It might have been," said the tall man grimly,

"if Sonya Damitri hadn't warned me."

Eric jammed on the brakes.

"Sonya?" he cried. "You mean we left her at the mercy of those devils?"

"No, she escaped. Step on it! I'll explain while I change."

The erstwhile vender pulled down the curtains and produced a make-up kit from a case on the floor of the cab. As he opened it and set to work, he crisply explained what had happened. Eric groaned.

"And to think she was that close! Why didn't you let me know?"

The other man's deft fingers were removing the wrinkles of age.

"She'd have been killed, and so would we," he replied. "As it was, she risked her life—and it was for you."

"If I could only get her out of the Invisible Empire!" the young Southerner said miserably.

The taller man was quickly swabbing the stain from his face.

"You'll never do that until the Yellow Doctor is dead. Her father is probably still a hostage at Yen Sin's base in China. Even if he isn't, you should know by now that the Doctor has many ways of forcing his agents to obey his orders."

Eric was silent, and the cab rolled on through the fog-shrouded streets. The man in the rear worked swiftly, with the skilled touch of a trained make-up artist. His yellow skin gave way to his natural color—a rich, even bronze, the deep-burned tan of a man who had spent years under blazing suns. His slitted eyes became straight, revealing themselves as dark-brown, and restless with a strange, vital power. In a few moments the features of the old Celestial were gone, even his yellowed hands. In the glass of the make-up kit showed the lean and whimsical face of Michael Traile, secret agent extraordinary, and leader in the fight against the Invisible Emperor.

HURRIEDLY, TRAILE shed the black Chinese joss suit and replaced it with a well-tailored gray from the case on the floor. Adjusting his shirt and tie, he peered out, saw they were going north on Kearny Street.

"Swing up to Grant Avenue," he said to Eric.

Eric looked around, startled.

7

"Back to Chinatown?" he exclaimed.

"Right! Sonya warned me to be out of Chinatown before midnight, and that means Doctor Yen Sin. It may be the break we've been waiting for."

"Say, there's something queer about this," Eric blurted out. "That was the message I was trying to give you—one from Army Intelligence. Colonel Manning called in at our Q-Station and said there was a rumor of something to be pulled off about midnight, near the Shan Low Gardens. He thought it might be connected with Doctor Yen Sin. The San Francisco police gave him the tip—Manning had told the chief about Yen Sin, as you suggested last night. They're going to have men planted, and Manning said he'd have Major Locke drive in from the Presidio to give us the details. He'll be parked on Gay, near Grant Avenue, at eleven-thirty."

"I don't like it," Traile muttered. "It looks like a trick of Yen Sin's. Turn at the next corner and park."

Eric complied, switched off the lights.

"What do you think is back of all this?" he asked tensely.

"I don't know," said Traile, "but the Shan Low Garden part may be a trap for us. It's possible that Yen Sin has learned we've had all our reports relayed through Army Intelligence. Letting this rumor leak out would be a good way to put us on the spot. We'll spot Locke's car and see if the Doctor is having it watched."

They left the cab and turned the next corner, climbing a slope toward Grant Avenue. They moved warily, taking advantage of the shadows and mist. The night seemed suddenly evil, oppressive with hidden menace.

"Keep your hand close to your gun," Traile said in an undertone. "We're still three blocks away, but there's a bare chance that we may have been followed."

Eric looked nervously over his shoulder.

"I swear, I'm getting so I even have nightmares about those yellow devils. I'll bet I didn't have five hours' sleep last night."

A faintly bitter smile touched Traile's lips.

"Wait till you've gone twenty-seven years without sleep, young fellow."

"Oh, hell!" said Eric contritely. "I'm sorry, Michael—I'd forgotten for a minute."

"It's all right." Traile was silent a moment. "I wonder how

much Sonya knows about that," he said in a musing tone. "She called me the 'Sleepless One' when she warned me tonight."

"She probably thinks you've found some queer drug to keep you awake, the same as Yen Sin believes."

"I suppose so," Traile said somberly. "It's just as well that they never learn the truth. I'd have been murdered long ago if the Doctor weren't so anxious to learn the secret of my going without sleep. He'd like to make use of it himself."

THEY WENT on through the misty street, moving as quietly as possible. Traile's keen eyes searched each shadow, scanned each passer-by, but his weary thoughts were on the strange affliction which had guided his life. He had been two years old at the time of that childhood accident in India. In an emergency operation, the lobe of the brain controlling sleep had been irreparably damaged, so that never again had he been able to lose consciousness. Only the flexibility of his young brain, and the training of a Yogi, had saved him from death through utter exhaustion. The Hindu miracle-man had taught him to relax his body completely for short periods, resting it as though in deepest sleep, even though his mind would always be awake. That had been the beginning of his odd existence. But there were few who knew his secret.

With that same faint bitterness, he recalled his peculiar boyhood, back in the States. His parents had employed a day and a night tutor, to keep his ever-wakeful brain busy with one subject after another. There had been a physical instructor to balance that strenuous mental life with games and sports. For a time it had been exciting—until he realized the vast gulf between himself and other boys.

Twenty-seven years without a single instant of forgetfulness! Twenty-seven years without shutting out life for even one blessed moment! It had made him a man apart, matured him before his time, made him a restless seeker after new hobbies, new ways to fill the long hours when others were sleeping and he was so desolately alone.

Hobbies, travel, new languages to study. It was a combination of these which had led him by accident into the web of the Invisible Empire, that vast criminal organization which was secretly spreading its tentacles over the world, under the guidance of the mysterious surgeon-mandarin, Doctor Yen Sin.

"We must be nearly to Grant Avenue," Eric's voice broke in on his thoughts. "Major Locke ought to be parked within half a block of here."

A blur from a street-light showed part of the corner as they approached it. Suddenly, from the murk beyond the light came a muffled snarl, like a cat growling in its throat. Traile instantly halted, one hand on Eric's arm.

"What's the matter?" whispered the younger man.

"Probably nothing—might be a signal between Yen Sin's men," Traile whispered back. Then his hand tightened on Eric's arm, for a strange figure had come out of the fog. It was a young woman—a woman of weird, dusky beauty. In her arms she held a black cat. Its tail was slowly switching from side to side, and its green eyes shone eerily in the glow of the street-light.

The woman paused, looked fearfully over her shoulder, then

gazed around into the mists. Traile drew back into the shadows beside Eric. The cat growled again deep in its throat, tried vainly to get free. Traile saw that its collar was secured by a length of fine silver chain to a band on the woman's left wrist.

In the same moment, he caught a strange aroma, an odor oddly disturbing to his senses. It seemed to arouse some half-buried memory. He sniffed again. It was a blending of odors, of cassia and resin, of drugs and spices—a queer mustiness, yet, at the same time, sickly sweet. He could not place it, yet it seemed to fit with that mysterious, sloe-eyed creature under the light.

A car passed by, and the woman hastily stepped back from the street-light. And in that moment, with the shadows obliquely crossing her weirdly beautiful face, Traile knew what it was she had brought to mind. A scene in Egypt, where he—

Bong! A distant clock struck the first note of twelve. The woman turned and stared into the fog. She seemed to be listening fearfully for something.

Bong! At the second stroke, the black cat gave a screech and leaped from the woman's arms. Tugging at the silver chain, it backed away, spitting and snarling. She reached down to draw it toward her—then abruptly stiffened.

Out of the gloomy night came a faint, unearthly song—an indescribable wailing, like ghostly music from the past. There was no trace of the singer, but the strange aroma of spices and drugs seemed to become stronger. As the throbbing music increased to a swifter tempo, the sloe-eyed woman took a jerky step forward, then a strangled cry burst from her lips.

A chill raced up Traile's back. The woman's face was twitching, queerly aging with every stroke of the clock. The eerie chant from nowhere rose to a higher pitch, as though the invisible singer stole closer in the fog. Under its weird spell, his brain seemed all but dazed.

The black cat gave a last tortured snarl and fell dead. But Traile hardly saw it, for his dazed eyes were fixed on the woman's face.

It was shriveling, darkening, the veins standing out lividly as that frightful metamorphosis went on. The woman's right hand flew up to her throat, and with horror he saw that it, too, had shrunken. For an instant it clawed as though some frightful, unseen thing were choking her to death. In amazement, he saw that her clothes were like scorched rags. She staggered back against the bronze lamp-post, and the misty light made a mirage about her head.

An icy horror swept over Michael Traile. Before his eyes, that strangely beautiful creature was turning into a mummy!

CHAPTER 2
THE WHITE SCARAB

A SECOND more, Traile's horror kept him rooted to the spot. He tried to move, but his legs seemed paralyzed, his body numbed by the shock of that terrible sight. The eerie song rose to a sudden, frenzied note and sharply ended. There was a moment of stark silence, then from out in the fog came a shrill scream. It was followed at once by three fierce blasts of a police whistle, from the opposite direction.

Released from his daze, Traile started toward the tottering figure by the light. Eric stumbled after him, and in a side glance he saw that Eric's face was deathly white. The trill of other whistles and the shouts of running men became audible from the direction of Gay Street. But the padding of stealthy feet gave him quick warning that other men were closer. He spun around, jumped away from the light.

Three grim-faced Chinese were rushing out of the mist, straight for the stricken woman. Behind them he dimly glimpsed two others carrying an ancient, coffin-like box.

"Look out, Michael!" Eric cried hoarsely.

Traile jerked the .38 from his armpit holster as he saw the first man's dagger. The Chinese drew back his arm for a swift throw. Flame spurted from Traile's gun, and the killer sagged in a grotesque heap. One of the others dived low, and Traile's hasty shot went over his head. With a squeal of triumph, the yellow man drove a knife up toward Traile's heart. Like a flash, Traile slammed the butt of his pistol down on the killer's head.

The Oriental groaned and fell, but his clutching hands dragged the American down. Traile heard Eric's angry yell, then the crashing report of two quick-fired shots. The night was suddenly alive with Chinese. Above their jabbering voices, and the increasing volume of whistles, as the police neared the spot, he heard a frightened cry in French. As he pulled himself free from the dying Chinese, he vaguely saw a man in evening attire fleeing into the night.

Two Orientals had seized the stricken woman, were dragging her to one side. The men with the long, queer box had brought it closer, and with a start Traile saw that it was a mummy-case. The Chinese were trying to force the woman into the coffin-shaped box.

Eric was down, struggling desperately with two of the assassins. As Traile sprang to help him, Eric pulled his gun-hand free. The weapon blazed, and one of the killers collapsed. Eric whipped the smoking barrel across the other one's face, scrambled to his feet. Together, he and Traile whirled toward the mummy-case. Just as they turned, the unfortunate woman fell to her knees, the hilt of a dagger protruding from her breast. In a cold fury, Traile triggered his gun. The man, who had stabbed her, plunged over the mummy-case, blood gushing from his mouth.

Eric swung, and another Chinese went down. Traile was leaping at the nearest killer, when he heard a rush of feet from behind. He pivoted swiftly. Off to the side, barely visible in the mist, he glimpsed the face of Sonya Damitri. She was crying out in desperate warning to Eric.

A tall, robed form had stepped from the murk. Traile went rigid. He was looking on the Satanic face of Doctor Yen Sin!

The Yellow Doctor's right hand was raised, exposing a poison-needle ring on his long-nailed index finger. The needle tip was almost at the back of Eric's neck!

FRANTICALLY, TRAILE swerved his still smoking gun. A snarling Oriental hurled himself between them, and the gun blazed in the killer's face. The man toppled back with half of his jaw blown off, and his crumpling body struck against Yen Sin. The Crime Emperor was thrown off his balance, and the deadly needle raked harmlessly down Eric's sleeve. Traile jumped to prevent a second attempt at murder.

A look of rage crossed the Yellow Doctor's face. With incredible swiftness, he sprang toward Sonya and threw the girl in front of him. Eric jumped forward with a stifled cry. The Crime Emperor gave a sharp command, and three yellow assassins dashed to his rescue. Traile lashed out, and the first man reeled back. A plunging Chinese struck at his knees from behind. He went down, but rolled over hastily, and the killer's knife grated into the pavement. Something hit the street-light with a shattering of glass. The light went out, but in a few moments a flashing beam probed through the mist.

The blue-clad form of a policeman appeared back of the torch, and pounding feet announced the nearness of others. Doctor Yen Sin and Sonya had vanished. A powerful engine roared, as a car hurriedly sped away, and Traile heard the foot-steps of fleeing assassins when the roar of the car had died out.

"What th' hell's goin' on here?" panted the officer who had arrived first.

Traile wheeled to Eric without answering. The young South-erner had a bruise on his face, and his clothes were disheveled.

"I'm O.K.," Eric said tensely, at Traile's hurried query. He looked around with an anxious gaze. "Did you see what happened to—"

Traile gave him a quick, warning look, and wheeled to face a barrage of questions, as more police appeared. A man of above medium height, with the authoritative air of one accustomed to giving commands, pushed his way into the group. Traile recognized the bristling brows and belligerent features of Major Jacob Locke, Army Intelligence officer.

The Army man turned to the sour-faced detective in charge. He spoke in a brusque but lowered voice.

"These two men are all right, Flaherty. They're the ones I was waiting for. Special detail from Washington."

"Yeah?" growled Flaherty, but his leathery face lost its look of suspicion as he gazed back at Traile. "Well, mister, what started this slaughter-house?"

Traile pointed into the shadows.

"Turn your light over there."

The detective played the beam over two dead Chinese, along a path of blood where it was obvious that a third body had been dragged. A few yards away lay the assassin who had fallen dead across the mummy-case. His body had evidently been pushed

The woman shriveled there before their very eyes as the night suddenly became alive with Chinese.

aside in a hasty but vain attempt of Yen Sin's men to make off with the stricken woman.

Locke's frosty blue eyes popped, and Flaherty swore, as the mummy-case itself became visible in the light. The lid was ajar, and gleaming through the crack was the hilt of the dagger with which the woman had been stabbed. As Flaherty tilted the flashlight, Traile lifted the lid and laid it aside.

"Holy mackerel!" muttered the detective.

Even Traile stared down in astonishment, prepared though he was. But for what he had already seen, he would have sworn he was looking down on an ancient mummy, wrenched from its winding-shroud. Not a trace of the woman's dusky beauty remained. Her face, like that portion of her body visible under the bits of rotted winding-strips, was old, dark and shriveled. The silver band hung loosely about her skinny wrist. He bent over, pulled at the fine linked chain, which like the band was tarnished.

It gave, and there in the light was all that remained of the cat—mummified and shrunken like its mistress. But its blackened teeth were still drawn back, as though in a soundless snarl at the thing which had caused its death.

FLAHERTY SHOVED his hat back on his head, looked around blankly at the others. Major Locke was still gazing with a look of stupefaction at the mummy, and the faces of the policemen mirrored his emotion. Flaherty turned helplessly to Traile.

"What th' devil did the Chinks want with this damn thing? And what's the idea of stickin' th' knife in it?"

"If I tell you the truth," Traile said grimly, "you'll say I'm insane. This mummy was a living woman not ten minutes ago."

Flaherty stepped back, his jaw hanging.

"Mister, you're crazy as hell!" He gazed down dazedly at the shriveled figure. "No, by God—it ain't possible!"

"I know that," said Traile. "But it happened."

He related briefly what he and Eric had seen. Major Locke gave an exclamation when he described the woman as they had first seen her.

"My God!" he said as Traile finished. "It must have been the girl we called 'Tanati!' The description fits her perfectly."

"Who was she?" Traile asked quickly.

The Intelligence major hesitated, looked around the group.

"I guess it can't make any difference now. She was believed to be an agent for some foreign power. We never could determine which one, nor her nationality. Our men have been watching her for some time—and I recall at least one report that she took mysterious trips into Chinatown, probably to meet another agent."

He started to add something, but the wail of a police siren interrupted. A riot car, followed by a machine with more detectives, drew up at the intersection. Spotlights dissipated the shadows, spread their glare over a small crowd of Chinatown residents which had begun to assemble. Police lines were quickly thrown about the scene. A third car halted nearby, and a haggard, middle-aged man hurried toward the mummy-case, followed by a uniformed police sergeant. Flaherty stepped into their path.

"Hold on Pete," he grunted at the sergeant. "Who's this guy?"

"My name is Meredith—Henry Meredith," the civilian said

in a harsh, but shaky voice. "I'm an archaeologist, and that mummy-case was stolen from me."

"The chief knows him, and he'd already phoned in about it, Lieutenant," interposed the uniformed man. "Then, when we got word about this—"

Flaherty stopped him with a curt gesture.

"Were these Chinks the birds that stole the case?" he demanded of Meredith.

"No, I think the men were Japanese," the archaeologist replied nervously. "Let me by, please. I want to see if they damaged the mummy."

"Hold on a minute," snapped Flaherty. "I got to get this straight."

But Meredith had already seen the shriveled figure in the pictograph-covered coffin. He darted forward, almost tripping over one of the dead Chinese.

"The vandals!" he groaned as he saw the dagger. "Why did they have to do this?"

He started to pull out the knife. "Let it alone!" grated Flaherty. He pushed the archaeologist back. "Now, let me get this right. You say that mummy was in the case when it was stolen?" Meredith's pallid face twitched. "Certainly, it was. But only part of the winding-strips had been removed. It's slow and careful work. Most of these strips have been torn loose by the robbers."

Flaherty glanced sourly at Traile and Eric.

"You better change your liquor, you two. A woman turned into a mummy!"

"What's that?" Meredith cut in, before Traile could reply.

"Just a funny story about how some dame did a presto-change act into that stiff," grinned the detective.

"Ridiculous!" the archaeologist snorted. "Your friend has been reading some cheap fiction about an Egyptian mummy curse."

Traile lit a cigarette, thoughtfully exhaled.

"Would you mind telling me," he asked, "how a mummy three thousand years old could bleed?"

MEREDITH STARTED, cast a quick look at the point where the dagger had entered. There was blood about the wound. Fear came back into his haggard face. "Good Heaven!" he said huskily. Then he seemed to brace himself. "It's obviously a silly trick. Anyone could have dipped the knife in blood first."

Traile bent over and unfastened the tarnished silver wrist-band.

"Would you say this dated back to the Twentieth Dynasty?" he inquired.

The other man stared at him, then at the curious hieroglyphics on the lid of the mummy-case.

"You're an Egyptologist?" he asked in an altered tone.

"I know a little about the subject," said Traile. He held up the band and the chain, with the mummified cat resting on the damp pavement. "Was this attached to the wrist of your mummy?"

"Yes—I think so," the older man said uncertainly. "There was an unusual lump under the winding-strips on the left side. It isn't uncommon to find pet cats or birds mummified, though they're mostly in canopic jars. I had only unwrapped as far as the neck. I stopped to examine that white scarab."

He pointed at the mummy's throat. Traile laid down the chain, stooped over the shriveled figure. The odor of resin and spices became stronger. He bent closer, gazing at the beetle-shaped amulet around the mummy's neck. An odd expression came into his dark eyes as he saw the small hieroglyphics carved in the base of the scarab. He glanced again at the pictographs on the mummy-case lid. On the head-section was a face in cartonage which resembled that of the mummy itself, except that the latter was shriveled. He looked back at the mummy's eyes, which showed like black beads through the shrunken lids. After a final inspection of the scarab, he stood up and turned to Meredith.

"You deciphered the warning?" he asked calmly.

The archaeologist hesitated, staring at the ground.

"Yes," he finally muttered, "but I'm not fool enough to believe in it."

Traile's bronzed face was expressionless.

"It's a curious coincidence, to say the least. Because—I actually heard the song."

Amazement leaped into Meredith's eyes.

"The death-chant of Amon-Ra?" he gasped.

Traile smiled a trifle dryly.

"Not having lived three thousand years ago, I can't swear to that. But it certainly had an uncanny sound."

"You said it!" put in Eric. "If a bunch of plantation hands had heard that, they'd be running yet."

Flaherty scowled at Traile and Meredith.

"Would you two mind lettin' me in on this confab?" he said with sarcasm. "What's this dope about a warning?"

"According to the inscriptions," Meredith reluctantly told him, "this mummy-case was made for the body of the Lady Ta-Nebit-Towy, chief chantress in the worship of Amon-Ra some time in the Twentieth Dynasty. Amon-Ra was the supreme god, or deity, of the ancient Egyptians. This warning has the usual phrase about a curse falling on grave-robbers or anyone who opens the tomb—but it has a peculiar addition evidently reserved for the sacred chantresses."

"Well, let's have it," grunted the detective.

"It says that the Lady Ta-Nebit-Towy will return to life, and will live for an appointed time, until the death-chant of Amon-Ra calls her back to her tomb to wait for her next reincarnation."

Two of the policemen edged away from the mummy-case, and Traile saw Major Locke stare at the blood around the dagger. Flaherty gazed dubiously from the mummy to Meredith.

"You believe that hooey?" he demanded.

Meredith wet his lips with his tongue.

"No," he said doggedly, "I've opened a dozen Egyptian tombs, and nothing has ever happened to me. I don't believe in curses or reincarnation. The old priests simply used those warnings to scare away grave-robbers."

"Yeah," said Flaherty. He scratched his jaw. "How much would that thing be worth now?"

"It's difficult to say," replied the archaeologist. "To a wealthy private collector, or a large museum, a mummy of this importance might be worth a hundred thousand dollars."

"Holy mackerel!" ejaculated the detective. "A hundred grand for a stiff! Well, that makes it a lot easier. The Chinks figured they'd grab it and fence it to some guy who'd pay that much."

"That's my opinion, too," muttered the archaeologist. "But I still believe the original robbers were Japanese."

"I was comin' to that," said Flaherty. "Just how and when did this happen?"

MEREDITH NERVOUSLY looked at his watch. Traile noted that the man's hands were shaking. "It was about eleven o'clock," the archaeologist began. "I was going down to my storehouse, a block or so from Dock Thirteen. I keep everything there from my excavations until it's sorted and packed for re-shipment to museums or collectors. When I got there I found my night watchman, Johnson, tied up and gagged. He said he had been knocked senseless by some men who broke in through a rear door. He had only a glimpse, but he was sure they were Japanese. He recovered consciousness before they left, and he could hear them whispering in the special room where I keep the mummies. But, of course, he did not understand the language."

"Funny, about this Jap business," grunted Flaherty. "He must've been mistaken. Lots of people can't tell 'em apart."

"There was a Jap in it, all right," interrupted one of the detectives. "I saw one haul out of here just as we hit the place. He had a nasty cut on the side of his head, so he must have been in the scrap."

"I get it," said Flaherty. "Some Japs stole the mummy, but these Chinks got wind of it and tried to hi-jack it. It's an open-and-shut case."

Traile nudged Eric to be silent as the young Southerner started to speak. But Major Locke spoke up.

"What about Tanati?" he demanded of Flaherty. "You're forgetting what these two men saw."

"Oh, no, I ain't," said Flaherty, with a sour grin. "I got it all doped out. They seen her in the fog, just about the time these Chinks tried to hi-jack the mummy. The dame beats it, scared of gettin' hurt, and meanwhile some Chink grabs out the mummy and is makin' off with it. A Jap tries to stop him and some John Chink lets fly with his knife—only he misses the Jap and stabs the mummy. That's what these birds saw, only they thought it was the dame."

"But they heard a queer death-chant!" said Locke stubbornly.

"Ever hear any Chink music?" said Flaherty. "It's queer enough to make your hair stand on end. The Greater Chinese Theater ain't far from here—they must've heard part of the show and couldn't tell where it was comin' from."

Michael Traile slowly nodded.

"That explains the whole thing, Lieutenant. It's easy enough to imagine something uncanny when things happen so rapidly."

"But—" said Eric, amazed. Then he closed his mouth.

Major Locke stared at Traile, and Flaherty complacently winked at one of his men.

"Guess that closes the books," he observed. "All we gotta do now is check up on these stiffs and try to get a lead on the rest of 'em."

Meredith broke in nervously.

"It's imperative that I get this mummy back to my storehouse. The damp air may have ruined it already."

"Hmm," said the detective. "It's evidence, but seein' the air might ruin it, maybe I can release it till we see if it's needed. Main thing, it ain't a corpse, anyway not the kind we got to bother about. But I'll be wantin' to ask your watchman some questions."

"You can go back with me now," agreed Meredith. His voice had a strained, yet eager note. "If I can find some means of transporting the mummy-case—"

"We'll grab off one of the morgue cars," said Flaherty. "They've got to wait till the coroner gets here, anyhow."

HE AMBLED off, and Meredith knelt to remove the dagger from the mummy's breast. Traile stooped to watch him. The archaeologist gingerly pulled out the knife, and they both bent over to look at the hole it had made. But the only blood was that around the narrow gash. Meredith stood up, wiped the blade with his handkerchief, and carefully eyed the weapon. Traile straightened after another inspection of the cut.

"Japanese dagger?" he said in a bored tone.

"Yes, it is," mumbled the archaeologist. "I happen to know a little about foreign weapons. The lieutenant simply had one little detail wrong. It was a Japanese who tried to stab one of the Chinese, and he struck the mummy by mistake."

"I tell you this mummy was a living woman not ten minutes ago."

Traile nodded carelessly, turned to Eric and Major Locke. They drew apart from the rest.

"Why did you lie to Flaherty?" Eric whispered.

"I'll explain later," Traile said in an undertone. He motioned to Locke, went on in the same lowered voice: "I want to be ready to follow Meredith, but without his suspecting it. If you'll slip away to the edge of the crowd, near your car, Eric and I will follow in a moment. Also, I've something important to tell you—connected with foreign espionage."

The fierce-looking Intelligence major lost his brusque manner.

"Espionage connected with this mummy affair?" he said in a startled voice.

"Not so loud," Traile cautioned him. "You never know when one of the Yellow Doctor's agents may be at your elbow."

"I'd like to know more about that devil," muttered Locke. "He may be the explanation of several puzzles in our Intelligence work."

"I'll tell you more later," said Traile. He waited until the other man had strode off through the crowd, then sauntered back toward Meredith. Flaherty had returned, and two policemen were waiting to carry the mummy-case to the morgue car. The archaeologist picked up the curiously painted lid, started to place it on the ancient coffin. A sudden, new fear came into his haggard face.

"The amulet!" he cried hoarsely. "It's gone!"

Traile looked at the mummy's throat. The scarab had vanished, and where it had been was only a yellowish spot. It had a sticky appearance.

"The damn thing must've slipped down into the box," grunted Flaherty.

"No, it couldn't have!" Meredith said in a harsh voice. "It was—"

"What's the matter?" asked Traile, as the older man broke off.

"Nothing," said Meredith thickly. He forced the lid down on the case. "Never mind the scarab," he told Flaherty. "It wasn't of any great value."

"Well, it's your baby, not mine," said the detective.

The two policemen picked up the mummy-case, lumbered off through the crowd. Traile and Eric Gordon slipped away to one side, found Major Locke and hurried to where the officer's car was parked. As they drove around the corner to Grant Avenue, they were just in time to see the black morgue machine start off into the mists.

"Did anything else happen?" asked Locke, as he followed the other car.

"Meredith's scarab disappeared," said Traile. He reached into his pocket, opened his hand under the dash light. The white amulet shone dully in the glow.

"Judas Priest!" Eric yelped. "You swiped it with all those cops looking?"

Traile smiled.

"Yes, but I think I'll add the art of stealing to my other hobbies. I almost muffed it."

"What do you want of that thing?" Locke said, staring at the scarab. "Do you think it has some secret meaning that will give you a clue?"

"A clue? Possibly," replied Traile. "But I already know the meaning."

"What does it say?" exclaimed Eric.

Traile gazed soberly at the inscription on the scarab.

"It says, 'Seek not the truth from the dead.'"

CHAPTER 3
DRAGON LORD OF CRIME

WITH ITS sinister hush, that strange black room was like some ancient tomb. The faint light failed to bring out the colors of the tapestries which covered the walls. It made them seem like dull, black cloth, as somber as the ceiling. There were no windows, nor any signs of an entrance.

It was a weird room, but stranger yet was the scene within its walls. On a large rectangular table was a miniature city, a model in careful detail of the city of San Francisco. Even to the green lawns of Golden Gate Park, the heights of Twin Peaks and Telegraph Hill, it was accurate in every point. Tiny electric lights shone in some of the miniature buildings—lights of various colors. Around the model city, the Bay was faithfully represented, including the jutting rock of Alcatraz.

At one end of the table bearing the miniature city sat a tall, robed figure. Like a living picture of Satan, a hideous yellow face looked down at the tiny buildings. The man's tawny eyes were drawn into narrow slits, the pupils contracted to black dots. It was a pointed, evil face—a face of ruthless power.

Though there were lamps on the walls, they were dark. The only light came from the tiny colored bulbs in the miniature buildings. In that mysterious room the effect was startling, as all perspective was lost. The miniature city seemed San Francisco itself, heavily shrouded in gloom. The impassive Chinese became a yellow giant, a mighty figure of evil crouching over the city.

An orange light flickered suddenly in one of the tiny buildings. The eyes of Doctor Yen Sin shifted to the spot. The building was a miniature replica of a pagoda-towered structure, almost in the center of a little Chinatown. Calmly, the Crime Emperor reached out a yellow hand. His long-nailed finger touched one of the several buttons recessed in the table.

"Observer Five," a voice spoke in Chinese from a hidden amplifier. "Situation unchanged. Police still questioning Meredith."

"What report on Michael Traile?" the Yellow Doctor asked tonelessly.

He spoke as though the observer were in the secret chamber. There was no sign of a microphone, but the quick reply showed that his question had been heard at once.

"Michael Traile is close by, with Eric Gordon and a third man with whom Traile has had conversation. He is possibly one of the Q-Unit."

"Describe this man," ordered the Crime Emperor.

"Not as tall as Traile, heavier built, with a military manner," reported the unseen spy. "Bristling eyebrows, large features, with a fierce expression and—"

"Enough," said Doctor Yen Sin. "The man is Major Locke, of American Army Intelligence. Assign an observer to mingle with the crowd and follow him if he separates from Traile."

"Yes, Master," came the hurried response.

"Inform me of further developments," ordered Yen Sin. He pressed a second button, and in another miniature building, not far from the tiny Chinatown, a green bulb winked.

"Number Eight," a low voice sounded from the hidden amplifier. "Negative reports from Buildings G, R, F and S. No reports yet from Buildings D and J."

The Crime Emperor's thin lips tightened.

"There has been sufficient time. Investigate the delay."

The green light went out. Doctor Yen Sin gazed impassively into space. Somewhere in the room, a muffled buzzer made a sound like the warning of a rattlesnake. The surgeon-mandarin touched a switch under the edge of the table, watched the wall at his right. A thin, vertical streak of light appeared against the darkness of the tapestries. It widened, revealing a door on which a section of one tapestry was cleverly affixed.

THE SLENDER form of a girl became visible in silhouette against the light. She came slowly into the dim chamber. Two stolid Orientals followed, and the secret door closed behind them. Lights on the walls, made in the shape of coiled serpents, suddenly blazed up and showed the girl's face. It was Sonya Damitri.

"You wished to see me?" she whispered.

The Yellow Doctor looked at her without expression, noting the hunted light in her black eyes, and her lips so red against the chalky pallor of her face.

"I am waiting for your report," he said tonelessly.

Under the hypnotic power of his eyes, she took a dragging step closer.

"My report?" she faltered. "You mean, why—"

Doctor Yen Sin smiled mirthlessly.

"I wish to know the details of your mission this evening, my dear Sonya. The period between eleven and the time when you joined me."

"I—I had almost forgotten," she whispered. "All this other—"

"Your report," said the Crime Emperor. His voice was gently mocking.

"I found a clue to the identity of Monsieur X," she said hurriedly. "I saw a man at the St. Francis Hotel—a man I am sure is an agent for France. I followed him into Chinatown. He went to the Shan Low Gardens, but I lost him there. I think he must have gone out by a hidden exit, or else to some private room."

"Your pursuit of this man did not lead you near Sacramento Street?" queried Doctor Yen Sin softly.

Sonya's eyes were wide with repressed emotion.

"No, I was not near there!" She made a desperate gesture. "Why do you torture me like this? I know you are going to punish me for keeping you from—"

"Continue your report," ordered the Yellow Doctor without expression.

35

The two guards leaped after her, seized her arms.

"There is nothing else," she said in a hopeless tone. "I left the Shan Low Gardens, came here and went with you as you directed."

Yen Sin's long fingernails tapped slowly on the table. He glanced past the girl at the immobile guards. When he went on, he changed from the Chinese language to Russian.

"It is most peculiar. Someone, with access to the latest observer, reports he learned that a certain nut vender was under suspicion of being my most dangerous enemy, Michael Traile. This person also learned that Eric Gordon was in Chinatown, disguised in some manner and aiding Traile in his attempts to discover my hiding-place."

The girl's lips were now almost bloodless. Doctor Yen Sin smiled with the same faint mockery.

"This person warned the two men of their danger just as Group Nine was about to close in. They escaped, and four of my trained men have been lost."

"I know nothing about it," Sonya said unsteadily.

The mockery went out of Yen Sin's eyes, and a furious rage blazed up in its stead.

"You are lying!" His yellow hand shot out, gripped her bare arm. As the sharp nails dug into her flesh, she moaned and tried to pull back.

"You warned them!" snarled the Crime Emperor. "And later when I was about to strike down that callow fool, you nearly caused my death to save him!"

Sonya's face was ashen, but her eyes shone with a sudden, wild light.

"Yes, I saved him! I would do it again! Now, kill me—have it ended!"

SHE HAD sprung toward him in her fierce outburst. The two guards leaped after her, seized her arms. For an instant longer, the murderous snarl twisted Yen Sin's lips. Then a film came over his tawny eyes, and the sardonic smile returned.

"No, my dear Sonya," he said in a silky voice, "you are too valuable a spy for me to sacrifice to a personal rage, I should have guarded against your sentimental folly."

Her eyes dilated with a slow, increasing terror which made her more beautiful than ever.

"You are playing with me," she whispered. "What do you mean to do?"

"I am going to trust you with one more mission." Yen Sin's hand dropped below the edge of the table. When it reappeared, it held a small poniard. He held out the weapon, hilt first. Sonya shrank back with a horrified expression.

"No! I will not do murder—even to save myself!"

The Yellow Doctor's eyes narrowed again.

"There is one whom you seem to have forgotten," he reminded her.

But a triumphant look came into her face.

"You can trick me no longer! I learned ten minutes ago that my father escaped from your men in Shanghai."

"Your honorable father will be retaken," Yen Sin promised her coldly. "He was aided by a traitor who was bought by Japanese gold. The Japanese expected to learn my secrets from your parent, but they have been disappointed. Someday the brown dogs will regret they did not start to investigate the Invisible Empire sooner."

The fury had partially returned to his eyes as he mentioned the race he hated equally with the Caucasian. Sonya waited, her expression a mixture of fear and defiance. After a minute, Yen Sin slowly lowered the poniard, beckoned to the guards to release her.

"Come closer, my child," he said suavely.

Reluctantly, she obeyed. The Yellow Doctor stood up, and his oddly filmed eyes gazed down into hers. A new, frightened look swept over her face. She took a step backward, then stood motionless. The pupils of Yen Sin's eyes suddenly enlarged to enormous size, until they were like black, bottomless pools. The girl swayed toward him. He stretched out one hand, touched her arm. A brief shiver ran over her slim body, then her eyes became glassy, dazed.

In a queer monotone, the Crime Emperor began to speak. The words were Russian, uttered in a soft, soothing cadence. The guards watched, fearfully. Yen Sin ignored them, never moving his gaze from the beautiful girl before him. A minute passed, and he still spoke. Gradually her tense attitude relaxed. A strange, dreamy smile filled her eyes.

Doctor Yen Sin waited. Half a minute passed, then the dazed expression began to fade from Sonya's face. In the precise instant when the Yellow Doctor saw the light of normalcy return to her eyes, he spoke.

"Closer, my child," he said, as he had spoken before that swift hypnosis. "I have decided to place you on probation."

For the fraction of a second, a look of uncertainty drew her arched brows together. The Crime Emperor went on as though no interval had elapsed.

"It is true that your father is no longer a hostage. But even if he is not recovered, there is one other whose life you value."

"You mean—Eric?" she said in a whisper.

Yen Sin coolly smiled.

"I shall rescind the order for my men to kill him if you swear to serve the Invisible Empire with no further attempt to escape."

Disbelief, hope, then misery flashed across her lovely face. Finally, she nodded.

"I swear it," she said in a low voice.

"You must make no attempt to see him again," Yen Sin said sternly. "On those terms alone, I shall forget what has happened."

There were unshed tears in her eyes, but she slowly moved her head. The Yellow Doctor spoke to the guards in Cantonese, touched the switch to open the secret door. As Sonya went out, her dark head bent, a cruel smile twisted his lips.

For some time after the swiveled panel closed, he watched the miniature city. The orange bulb which had first lit up finally blinked out a signal. The Crime Emperor answered, gave instructions in Chinese. He had hardly disconnected the circuit when the green light in the pagoda-roofed building flickered violently.

"Number Eight!" the agent's tense voice came as Yen Sin touched a button. "Master, we have discovered a terrible thing!"

"The secret?" demanded the Yellow Doctor.

"No, Master. It is still unknown. But I sent men to Building D. We found why there had been no report. It was because—"

An eerie, wailing chant came through the amplifier in the secret room. The Crime Emperor sprang to his feet, a look of alarm on his saffron face. The weird song was choked off as abruptly as it had begun. Yen Sin bent hastily over the row of buttons.

"Number Eight!" he said. "Number Eight!"

Only an ominous silence answered his anxious call. He straightened, stared at the miniature Chinatown. The green signal light was dark.

CHAPTER 4
THE GIRL IN THE COFFIN

THE FOG had deepened, and Major Locke was forced to drive at a snail's-pace as he followed the morgue car. "But why did you go back on your first story?" he asked Traile.

Traile looked absently into the misty night.

"I wanted the police to think it an ordinary theft—also the reporters. There's some deep significance to the whole thing— something sinister. We may discover it this way."

"Meredith seemed to be hiding a desperate fear," Locke muttered. "I wonder what he knows."

"I don't think he knows the entire truth," Traile said thoughtfully, "but he should lead us to it."

"You said this had some espionage connection," observed Locke. "I don't see how it could."

41

"I meant Doctor Yen Sin, first." Traile lighted a cigarette, inhaled deeply. His bronzed face was grim in the reflected glow of the headlights as he went on. "I've given you only a sketchy idea of the Invisible Empire, Major—though Colonel Manning may have told you the full details I gave him."

"No, he didn't," said Locke. "I've been busy on another affair."

"The Invisible Empire contains probably the largest group of trained agents of any organization in the world," said Traile. "It is an international league, essentially criminal, though the Doctor has certain political motives in the back of his head—an intention to drive Japan out of China, become ruler of the East, and eventually challenge the supremacy of the white race."

"Good God!" said Locke in a startled voice. "You really believe it's possible?"

"Over a period of time, yes. The man is an evil genius, and his Invisible Empire combines not only criminals and spies but their victims. On its rolls are murderers, crooks of every degree and almost every nationality, and espionage agents he has literally stolen from foreign powers—or bribed. But the crafty part is the addition of his blackmail victims. He is a wizard at finding the dark spots in a person's life. And be doesn't stop at bleeding his victims for money. If they are powerful politically, or have certain valuable knowledge, he forces them to turn that power or knowledge to his use."

"But I don't see why someone hasn't given him away long ago," objected Locke.

"He rules by fear—and torture. The ramifications of the Empire are tremendous. I doubt if ten people, even his chief

agents, know the entire workings of the scheme. The main secrets the Doctor keeps locked up in his cunning brain. Don't underestimate him—he has the ability of a dozen brilliant men, and his knowledge of modern science is only equaled by what he knows of ancient secrets."

"That blond girl who gave us the slip three nights ago—the one you called Iris Vaughan," said Locke. "You think she was one of his spies?"

"Quite certain," answered Traile. "We discovered that in Washington. She was connected with the British Embassy, but serving him secretly. He has a terrific hold on her because of the opium habit she has acquired. I think he cleverly keeps her deprived of the drug at times to make her to do what he wishes. He has other tricks to force the rest to obey him."

"I wonder why he was there tonight?" conjectured the Intelligence major. "You said he seldom took a personal part in the physical workings of his schemes."

"Only when it's extremely important," said Traile. "But he

and his agents weren't the only ones present. That's what puzzles me. It's obvious that at least one Japanese was also hidden in the fog, waiting to see something. He may have been one of the Jap merchants who have recently forced their way into Chinatown, but I suspect they are also spies for the Mikado."

"You're right on that," growled Locke. "We've been watching every one of them. We had an anonymous tip that they were up to something crooked."

Eric leaned over from the back seat. "What about that fellow in evening clothes, Michael? You saw him, didn't you, just before the police came?"

Traile tossed his cigarette out of the window.

"I caught only a faint glimpse. But I know one thing—he was a Frenchman." Locke sat bolt upright. "A Frenchman! Are you sure of that?" Traile smiled ironically. "At least, he was quite familiar with certain French oaths. Why?"

"Because," said Locke tautly, "that's the affair I've been working on for months—the mystery of a super-spy known as 'Monsieur X.'"

"How much do you know about him?" Traile asked quickly.

"We know he's a Frenchman, of course," said Locke.

He peered ahead for a moment, made a turn as the morgue car swung into the deeper mists near the Embarcadero.

"However, it's certain that he doesn't represent France," he went on. "From what we've been able to pick up, he deals in stolen military and naval information and plans—selling them to the highest bidder. We have absolute proof that he's dealt with Germany and Japan, and we're pretty sure he has sold information to half of the other foreign powers."

"Say, maybe he's just a go-between for Yen Sin!" exclaimed Eric.

"That's an idea," admitted Major Locke. "But we've run up against a blank wall in our efforts to locate him. He's operated down at San Pedro, the Navy base, and on the East Coast, and at half a dozen other places in the last three years. I've been detailed on that case alone, but he always seems to know just when my men and I are about to catch up."

Traile gazed out into the murk.

"That complicates it even further," he muttered. "From what you say, I don't think he's working with Yen Sin. The Yellow Doctor wouldn't permit any agent of his to become such a powerful figure—even as a phantom Monsieur X. That means there were at least three opposing forces near that corner tonight. The mummy of the chantress must have been of vital interest to all of them. Or else—"

"The morgue car's stopping," Eric broke in.

Locke instantly swung toward the curb.

"No, drive on by!" Traile clipped out. "Flaherty will suspect, otherwise."

Locke drove a hundred feet farther, parked around a corner, and they started back noiselessly into the fog.

"I want to get near enough to hear the watchman's story," Traile said in a low tone. "Perhaps we can find a window."

BUT THE words were barely ended when a cry of alarm sounded from the building the others had just entered. Traile

broke into a run, Eric and Locke close behind him. He reached the door of Meredith's storehouse, a small structure between gloomy shipping offices. The door was open, and by the light

Instead of the shriveled features and taped head of a mummy, they saw the pretty features of Iris Vaughan.

within he saw Flaherty dashing into a room adjacent to the first.

Without formality, Traile raced after him, his hand on the automatic in his shoulder harness. Flaherty jerked around, as Traile plunged through the second doorway.

"What the hell?" he erupted. Then he recognized Traile and saw Eric and Major Locke. With an angry snort, he turned back to the distraught archaeologist "All right, mister. Now what—"

He stopped, and Traile saw the dead man on the floor at Meredith's feet. He was lying crumpled up a few yards from an Egyptian canopic jar, and it was plain that he had died from the ugly stab wound in his side. Beyond him were more of the painted jars, and one side of the room was littered with ancient weapons and objects from excavations in various countries. Three large mummy-cases stood upright against the wall, two of them open.

Meredith had dropped down by the dead man, was shaking him as though by the very violence of his efforts he would bring him back to life. Flaherty pulled him away.

"Too late for that, mister. He's done for."

"Johnson—poor old Johnson!" Meredith said in a broken voice. "Oh, God—and I caused his death!"

"What's that?" the detective said sharply.

"I should never have left him here alone," groaned Meredith. "After what happened, I should have known they'd come back—"

"Why?" snapped Flaherty.

"The mummies—they've taken two more of them," the archaeologist said dully. Then for the first time he saw Traile and the others. A slow, angry red came into his face.

"Why have you followed us here?" he flung out harshly. "You're not police! Why are you prying into—"

A thudding sound, apparently from the floor above, made him break off. Flaherty spun around, revolver in hand.

"Where's the stairs?" he fired at Meredith.

"Through that rear door—to the left, gasped the archaeologist."

Flaherty seized Locke by the arm.

"Come on—I may need help. The rest of you guys look around down here."

He and the major dashed out, and their feet were heard clumping on the stairs. Traile started into the rear room, then suddenly turned back.

"What is it?" Meredith asked nervously.

Traile motioned him to keep still, took a noiseless step toward the three mummy-cases. The ones on the ends had been uncovered and their lids placed aside. The interior cases were also open and empty. But the lid of the middle coffin was still in place. He reached out, felt a wide space between the case and the lid. Lifting his .38, he gripped the edge of the lid with steely fingers. A quick jerk, and it came away.

A woman's voice gasped, and the light shone on hair like fine-spun gold. Traile slowly lowered his gun. Instead of the shriveled features or the taped head of a mummy, he was looking on the pretty face of Iris Vaughan!

ERIC AND the archaeologist were staring in astonishment

at the girl. She cowered back, her blue eyes wide in panic. Traile smiled with a tinge of irony.

"A poor hiding-place, Miss Vaughan."

Her lips trembled with a pathetic plea.

"Don't judge me yet," she whispered. "I came here merely—"

It was only a faint change, a brief narrowing of her luminous eyes—but it gave Traile warning. He whirled at lightning speed, then leaped aside. From the shadows near the rear door, a huge figure was stealing forward. In his uplifted hand was one of the ancient swords.

The man's grim face contorted with rage as Traile spun about. He sprang, and the heavy blade hissed down at Traile's head. Traile dived to the left and fired. The other man jerked under the bullet's impact into his shoulder. With a furious curse in Polish, he shifted hands on the sword. The ancient weapon flashed upward.

There was a pop, a splintering of glass, and the electric light went out. Traile fired again in the gloom. The powder flash showed the hulking Pole bent over, running toward the door from which he had entered. Then the blackness of the rear room swallowed him up.

Someone bumped against Traile, and he felt Iris Vaughan try to push on past. He swung her back to where Eric stood, half visible in the light from the front room.

"Hold onto her!" he rapped. "And keep out of that light."

A clatter of boots on the stairs announced Flaherty's hasty descent, then the detective's torch lanced through the dark. The edge of the beam momentarily shone on the injured Pole as he plunged through a doorway at the back of the storehouse.

"Halt!" bawled Flaherty. He dashed after the fleeing man.

"Be careful!" Traile shouted after him. "There may be others outside!"

But the detective charged on. They heard his revolver blast out two quick shots, heard his angry bellow for the fugitive to halt. Traile wheeled to Major Locke.

"Guard that rear door. He and the girl were probably alone, but we'll take no chance of another surprise. Eric, watch the front door, but stay back out of sight."

"What about—" Eric made a hasty grab at Iris Vaughan's hand. "No, you don't!"

Traile crossed the room, bent over to look at the thing which Eric had taken from the girl's fingers.

"It's only a hotel key," said Eric, holding it up in the dim light.

Traile took it, then stooped and picked up a small vanity bag which the blond English girl had tried to kick out of sight. He tumbled out its contents in his hand. There were some bills, a compact and a coin-purse. In the purse he found a folded slip of paper.

He read the penciled words: " 'Paul Greenwood, photo third from left, bottom row, Camera Portrait display.' "

He heard a sharply drawn breath, but the sound did not come from Iris Vaughan. He looked up, Locke was staring at Meredith, and he saw the archaeologist's twitching lips.

"What do you know about Paul Greenwood?" he asked.

Meredith looked at him sullenly.

"I don't know anything about him."

"Sure of that?" asked Traile.

"Certainly," snapped Meredith. "I never even heard of him before."

Traile came a step nearer.

"Then, perhaps," he said softly, "you have heard of the Invisible Empire?"

Meredith's already pallid face slowly drained of all color.

"No," he replied in a hoarse, desperate voice. "No, I don't know what you're talking about."

Traile's bronzed face hardened.

"You're a poor liar, Meredith. I advise you to tell the truth—before it's too late."

"What do you mean?" whispered the archaeologist.

"You're an accessory to murder," said Traile.

The last, flagging spirit seemed to go out of the other man. He staggered back, clutching at a mummy-case for support. Then, with an almost miraculous change, he jumped past and hurled the heavy case off balance. The ancient coffin crashed to the floor, forcing Traile to leap back. Before he could spring over it, Meredith was gone, taking the same route of escape the mysterious Pole had used.

CHAPTER 5
THE DEATH-CHANT
OF AMON-RA

L OCKE HAD started after Meredith in the same moment as Traile. They collided in the darkness of the rear room and sprawled to the floor. As Traile jumped up, he heard Iris struggling to get past Eric and reach the front of the building.

"Give me your car keys, then try to catch Meredith," he directed Locke. "I'm going to follow that other lead before Yen Sin can block it."

The Intelligence major mumbled a reluctant assent and hurried out into the fog. Traile returned to the mummy-room.

"Let me go," Iris was pleading with Eric. "I saw you help Sonya escape, that night in New York. I am no more guilty than she is."

Traile interposed curtly.

"You've had at least one chance to break away from the Doctor. I'll give you one more, if you'll help us."

"If I betrayed him, I'd be tortured—killed!" she moaned.

Traile gave her the vanity bag, took her arm and nodded to Eric.

"Come on, well have to move fast. That Pole may have warned Yen Sin already."

He put out the light in the front room, and they halted for a second at the doorway. The street was practically hidden by mist from the Bay. There was no sound except the mournful blast of a foghorn somewhere off in the night.

"Where are we going?" Eric whispered, as they went along the damp walk.

"Don't talk," muttered Traile.

He found Locke's car, swiftly examined the interior to be sure it was empty. In a few seconds they were inside, with Iris between Eric and him on the front seat. As the car rolled slowly through the mists, the blond girl looked fearfully around at Traile.

"What are you going to do with me?"

"That depends on you," he said. His dark eyes rested for an instant on her face, as it showed in the dash-lamp's glow. Except for her too bright eyes, she showed none of the effects of the opium habit. Her skin was still firm and clear; the ugly sallowness of the helpless addict had not begun to appear.

"What happened to Tanati?" he shot at her.

She stared at him in apparently true amazement.

"I don't know what you're talking about."

"Maybe you know why you were at Meredith's place," he said dryly.

She gazed down at her lap, fumbling restlessly with the vanity bag.

"I went there to take him a message," she replied unwillingly.

"What was it?" Traile persisted.

"Just three words, 'She is safe.' That's all I know."

Traile slowed to read a street sign, turned toward Market Street.

"Who did the Doctor mean by 'she'?"

The girl shook her pretty blond head.

"I don't know. I don't even know that it was from—*him.*"

"And, of course," Traile said elaborately, "you don't know anything about the man named Greenwood."

She opened her compact, nervously dabbed powder on the tip of her nose. He thought he felt her tremble.

"If I tell you," she said in a strained voice, "will you promise to keep me from being arrested?"

"Will it lead to trapping Yen Sin?" Traile countered.

"Yes," she said. Her voice was barely audible. "But you must swear to protect me against—the Doctor."

Traile looked searchingly at her. Her hands were tightly clenched in her lap and her eyes closed as though under the stress of some powerful emotion.

"I promise you will be safe," he told her grimly.

"Then"—she took a deep breath—"here is the answer!"

One hand flew up, and the compact swiftly snapped open. A cloud of pepper flew into the air. Sneezing, instantly blinded, Traile slammed on the brakes. He heard Eric give a yelp of pain, then the girl was gone from beside him. He threw the gear lever to neutral, snatched out toward her in spite of the agony in his eyes. But his hands closed on empty air.

"Good-night, Mr. Traile!" her voice floated back, on a note of malicious laughter. "Thank you for your protection."

TRAILE SWORE under his breath, felt his way out the left side of the car. Eric was stumbling around on the other side, sneezing and groaning. Traile took his handkerchief, wet it from the mist which had collected on the car windows. Tearing the cloth in two, he felt his way around and handed a piece to Eric.

"Here, swab your eyes. It may help some."

"The little devil!" Eric howled. "Here I am feeling sorry for her, and she blinds me and pushes me out in the street."

He sneezed indignantly.

"I should have known she was up to some trick," Traile said in a savage tone.

He wiped his smarting eyes, dampened another corner of the cloth and repeated the operation. But it was two or three minutes before he could see anything, and even then the pain was excruciating.

"Get in," he said to Eric, who had at last stopped sneezing. "We can't wait any longer. She'll warn the Doctor as soon as she can, and we've got to reach that hotel first."

"What do you think you'll find there?" Eric asked glumly.

"I'm not sure. Something important, or she wouldn't have tried so hard to get rid of the key and that bag."

Eric groaned ruefully.

"I wish she'd succeeded, the little hellcat!"

"Lean out around the wind shield," suggested Traile. "The mist may help a little."

His voice held a tired note, for the swift action of the past hour had depleted his reserve of strength. This was the Achilles heel of his peculiar physical make-up—the need for frequent relaxation periods to restore the energy he was constantly using up. Without such relaxation, he would sink closer and closer to the point of absolute exhaustion—a state of near paralysis. He had experienced it a few times, and had tried to guard against it ever since.

As they neared Market Street, he pulled the car over to the curb and climbed from under the wheel.

"Take it, Eric," he said wearily. "I'm getting close to the edge—I'll have to recharge my battery."

"Sorry, Michael," Eric said quickly. "I should have thought of it myself."

He took the wheel, and the car purred across Market, heading in the direction of Nob Hill. Traile stretched his long arms, lay back against the seat, forcing his tired muscles to relax their tension. A brief languor stole over him, a welcome peace and respite from all strain. This was his sleep.

ERIC PULLED a briar from his pocket, dumped tobacco into it while steadying the wheel with his elbow. The flare of his match lit up his ruddy face, and Traile saw that, in spite of all that had happened, the young Southerner still had his genial, boyish look. He smiled a trifle bitterly to himself. But for his childhood accident, he, too, might have been like that. There was only a slight difference in their ages—Eric was about twenty-five—but in his own strange existence he seemed to have lived forever.

His mind went down the long vista of sleepless years, over the problems he had met—the constant seeking for new interests, the eternally keeping busy, dreading the curse of boredom which came with the slightest empty period.

"What are we going to do when we get there?" asked Eric. "Bust on in—or wait for help?"

"We'll try to work it alone," said Traile. His voice was slow, lazy, as it always was when he was fully relaxed. "I'm sorry, though, that we haven't contacted the local F.B.I. before now. We might need their help."

Eric puffed at the briar.

"I still don't see why we've been working only through Army Intelligence, when I got all those direct wires hooked up to the other places."

"Yen Sin's agents tapped the Bureau wires in Washington, remember?" Traile replied. "He would probably expect us to work with the Department of Justice here. I used our Army connection, thinking it was the one the Doctor would least suspect."

Eric shook his head.

"That fellow Locke strikes me as kind of dumb. It'd be just too bad if he ever let it leak out that the Q-Unit is only a name covering your hook-up with the five departments—instead of being the five agents Yen Sin has been looking for."

"Locke doesn't know that," said Traile. "He thinks I'm just Q-3, the agent detailed to guide the Army on the Invisible Empire case."

Eric grinned.

"So that's what he meant when he asked me my number. He thinks I'm another Q-man."

Traile's dark eyes had a grave look.

"I'm afraid, Eric, I've let you in for as much danger as myself.

The Doctor may think the same thing. You've done a fine job on our secret communications, but I should never have let the Government borrow you from your company."

Eric glanced sidewise through the smoke from his pipe, and his ruddy face for an instant lost its boyishness.

"Don't worry about me, Michael. Even if it weren't for Sonya, I'd stick. I hate Yen Sin and the Invisible Empire as much as you do."

Traile slowly nodded.

"I know—but I'll feel a lot better when you're out of this mess."

"That won't be until Yen Sin's finished!" Eric said with determination.

The car swept along through the mists, which gradually thinned as they skirted Chinatown and climbed the heights to Nob Hill.

"There's the Fairlawn Hotel," said Traile. He sat up with an abrupt change of manner. All his weariness had gone, and his bronzed face was now fresh and alert. Eric looked at him with open envy.

"I wish I could get the hang of that trick. You look as though you'd had a full night's sleep, and here I am tired as a dog."

Traile grimly shook his head.

"Be thankful you don't have to do it. Sometime you'd give anything in the world, just to shut out life for even one short hour."

ERIC PARKED the machine not far from the main entrance, and they went on into the lobby. Traile carelessly jingled the key he had taken from Iris Vaughan, and led the way to the elevators. A sleepy operator glanced at the key. Traile kept the numbered disk covered in his hand.

"What floor, sir?" yawned the man.

"Nine," said Traile.

The lift man took them up, went down again. Traile halted midway of the hall into which he had started.

"Other direction," he whispered to Eric. "Room Nine-thir-ty-five."

The thick carpet deadened their footsteps as they approached the door. There was a *Do Not Disturb* sign hanging from the knob. Traile slipped his gun from under his coat, waited until Eric had done the same. Cautiously, he inserted the key and turned it. Standing aside, he twisted the knob and threw the door open.

A green lamp was shining on a writing desk in one corner. There was no sign of anyone in the room. Traile waited, then stepped inside. A connecting door to the next room was open, and the lights were on. He signaled for Eric to search the closet and the bath of the first room, while he covered the other doorway. Eric tiptoed back in a moment, shook his head.

Traile warily entered the adjoining room. It, also, was empty. On the dresser was a bottle of Scotch. Two empty glasses and a siphon stood on a table. A slight breeze blew the drapes at the sides of the window. A woman's traveling-bag and a smart overnight case rested on the luggage-stand.

"Looks like we've drawn a blank," said Eric.

He had hardly spoken when a muffled scratching was audible

from the closet. Traile motioned him to one side, unlocked the door and gave it a quick jerk. A solidly built youth about nineteen years old, lay half doubled up on the floor, bound expertly. Two wide strips of surgical adhesive tape were plastered over his mouth, covering the entire lower part of his face. The hopeful look in his eyes changed to alarm as he saw their automatics.

"Lock the door of the first room," Traile said to Eric.

He knelt and began to untie the young prisoner's bonds. In a few minutes, the lad was free. Traile helped him up, guided his unsteady feet toward a chair.

"I'll let you pull off those pieces of tape," he said. "Make it as quick as you can—we'll have to talk fast."

The boy gave him a weak nod, gingerly plucked at the tape. Eric had returned, was waiting beside Traile. In a moment, the boy's lips were free, and a handsome but immature face was revealed. Just now it was badly frightened.

"Are you Paul Greenwood?" Traile asked crisply.

"Yes, sir," said the boy, in a husky voice. He stared at Traile's gun.

"We're Government agents," Traile explained. He shoved the .38 under his coat. "It's vital that we know why Doctor Yen Sin had you captured."

Paul Greenwood gazed up blankly. "Who?" he asked.

"The Chinese mandarin known as Doctor Yen Sin," said Traile. "Maybe you've heard of him as the Invisible Emperor?"

"I never heard of him at all," declared the boy. A flush came back into his handsome young face. "All I know is that I was fool enough to let a girl get me up here and give me a drug or something." Traile eyed him sharply. To all appearances, the lad was telling the truth.

"Tell me what happened," he said, "as briefly as possible."

PAUL GREENWOOD fidgeted, looked at the signet ring on his hand. "That's all there was to it," he returned. "I registered here about eight o'clock. I'd just come in from Omaha. I went into the coffee-shop for a bite, and pretty soon a swell-looking blonde came in and took the next table. I—well, she—"

"I understand," said Traile, dryly. "What happened after you got acquainted?"

"She said she had a bottle of Scotch up in her room. I came on up with her. We had one drink—and that's all I remember until I woke up and found myself in that closet."

"And you've no idea why this happened?" Traile demanded.

The boy stopped rubbing his chafed wrists.

"I suppose so she could grab my money," he said gloomily. He took out his wallet, looked surprised as he counted the few bills it contained. "That's funny—she didn't steal a cent."

Traile took a turn back and forth, his bronze face deeply puzzled.

"Look here," he said abruptly, "I'm going to tell you the truth. For some reason, you were captured by the most dangerous criminal league in existence—a league headed by a powerful Chinese."

Paul Greenwood gazed at him in astonishment.

"But why would they want to capture me? I'm not rich."

"There's some reason," insisted Traile, "and you'll have to think of it. You're in danger right now."

The boy lunged up from his chair.

"Then I'm going to call the police!"

Traile calmly pushed him back.

"I'll have protection for you in a few minutes. Eric, get on that phone in the other room and call Hemlock Four-four-o-o. Give them my identification number, and tell them to rush a squad up here."

Eric disappeared. Traile turned back to the alarmed youngster.

"Try to think! There's a powerful motive for all this. Why did you come to San Francisco?"

"To meet my uncle," mumbled the boy. "When he visited us last week he said he might get me a job here for the rest of the summer vacation."

"Where's your uncle now?" asked Traile.

"I don't know. He telegraphed me to come here and wait for him—maybe he called my room while I was tied up in that closet."

"Have you that telegram?" Traile inquired.

"Yes, sir." The boy fished a folded yellow slip from his wallet. Traile ran his eyes over the message—

Paul Greenwood, 910 Becking Street, Omaha, Nebr. Position secured for you. Take noon plane to San Francisco. Register Hotel Fairlawn. Will meet you this evening. Please bring suitcase I forgot last week. Regards.

Uncle Cyrus.

Traile slowly looked up from the message.

"What kind of position was this?"

"I think I was to help him, maybe," hazarded Paul Greenwood. "He didn't say much, but I think he was expecting to get a job himself, and he thought he might work me in for a few weeks."

Traile's dark eyes studied the boy's face.

"What was your uncle's profession?"

Paul looked at him helplessly.

"I don't even know that. He hadn't visited us but once in nine years. He lived mostly in Chicago, I think. My mother said he made a lot of money during the War, doing something for the Government—but he never talked much about it. And he lost most of the money in the stock-market crash."

He paused, as Eric Gordon's voice was raised in argument in the next room. Traile listened for a second, eyed the telegram again.

"Was there anything valuable in that suitcase?"

The handsome youngster grinned.

"You couldn't get two bucks at a pawnshop for the whole works. All he had in it was an old suit, an alarm clock, and half a dozen old books."

"Where's the suitcase now?" Traile asked quickly.

"I checked it down in the lobby." The boy felt in his coat, and searched his other pockets. "Gosh, the ticket's gone!"

TRAILE WHEELED toward the phone, but in the same moment Eric appeared from the other room. "You'll have to talk to them, Michael," Eric said. "They think I'm trying to pull a fast one on them."

Traile took Paul Greenwood's arm and assisted him to the chair beside the phone stand.

"Call the night porter! Find out if the suitcase is gone, who took it and when!"

"Yes, sir," the boy said, eying him uneasily.

Traile hurried into the other room with Eric.

"Close that connecting door," he said in a low tone. "Then go watch to see he doesn't slip into the hall. I think his story is straight, but I'm not sure."

Eric shut the connecting door and surreptitiously peeped out into the corridor. Traile picked up the phone.

"Q-5," he said. "Who's on the line?"

"This is Agent Dodd," replied a nasal voice. "But how do I know you're Q-5?"

"You've a confidential order from Director Glover," Traile interrupted rapidly. "It's dated May Nineteenth, Special Code Number Q-5-8983. It contains a copy of a right index finger-print, and orders to cooperate implicitly with the man whose finger matches that print. Right?"

"Yes, but—" began the F.B.I. Agent.

"I'm that man," said Traile. "I want a squad at the Fairlawn as fast as you can make it. Bring that fingerprint—I'll match it!"

"All right, but if—" the agent's voice changed to a faint, whispering note, died out completely.

Traile rattled the hook, stared around at Eric. "Something just happened to the phone."

Then he saw the tense expression on Eric's face. He jumped up.

"What's the matter?"

"Listen!" Eric said hoarsely. "Don't you hear something?"

Traile felt a queer prickling at his scalp. It was not so much a definite sound, as a feeling of something evil in the air—something his ears could not really hear, but which a sixth sense told him was near. Then it came—a faint, quavering song, slowly rising into the eerie, throbbing wail he had heard once before that night.

The death-chant of Amon-Ra!

Above the wordless song came a sharp tinkling, as of broken glass. It seemed to come from the other room. Traile sprang to the door. It was locked. As he threw himself against it, he could feel the panel quivering from the vibrations of the mysterious chant.

"Help me break this open!" he rapped at Eric.

They hurled themselves against the door. A panel cracked, but the lock held. The weird, throbbing chant rose to a peak of frenzy. Then it swiftly died away, until there was only the faint, tremulous song which had been heard at first.

At their third onslaught, the lock broke, and the door burst open. Traile caught himself, swung around for a quick glance. Then he halted, amazed. For handsome young Greenwood had vanished, and there in his chair sat a weird, mummy-like creature. It was from the lips of this queer figure that the quavering melody came.

An instant more, Traile stared blankly. Then he saw the

tarnished signet ring which the creature wore on one wrinkled, leathery hand. He bent, stared in horror at that wizened face.

Like Tanati, Paul Greenwood had become a living mummy!

CHAPTER 6
THE MAN CALLED "X"

ERIC HAD stopped, white and sick, as he saw the crooning horror in the chair. "My God!" he whispered. "It's happened again! Look at him!"

Traile bent over the pitiful figure, gently shook its arm.

"Paul!" he said huskily. "Paul, can you understand me?"

No light of intelligence came into the creature's lusterless eyes. He made no attempt to resist when Traile pulled the chair away from the window and then lifted him onto the bed. But his shrunken lips still trembled in that weird and uncanny song.

"Look at his right hand!" Eric burst out.

Traile glanced down. The hand was white, bloodless. It showed no signs of the gruesome shriveling which had attacked the left. But the right side of Greenwood's face was almost as dark and shrunken as the other. Traile started to undress the stricken boy, then paused.

"Call the desk—get the house doctor!" he told Eric.

But before Eric could reach the phone, two men came running in from the other room. Traile straightened with a jerk.

"There they are, Brodie!" shrilled the first of the pair. He was a bald little man, evidently the night-clerk.

A paunchy man with a derby lumbered past him, then froze with a look of horror as he saw Greenwood.

"Don't stand there!" snapped Traile. "He may be dying. Get a doctor!"

The night-clerk backed away from the bed, his pop-eyes fixed on the quavering, shriveled figure.

"Good Heavens! It's the plague! We'll be ruined!"

His voice rose hysterically. Traile gestured to the half-stunned house detective.

"Close that window. If your house guests hear all this racket, there'll be a crowd up here in five minutes."

The note of command in his voice brought action. Brodie shut the window, picked up the phone.

"It don't work," he said stupidly, after a moment.

"Then go downstairs and phone the nearest hospital," Traile ordered.

"Wait!" the little clerk cried, as the house detective started out "Make these men explain this, and what they're doing here."

Traile produced the gold F.B.I. shield which he sometimes used when working as Q-5.

"I'm from the Department of Justice," he said to Brodie. "Hustle and get the doctor, will you?"

The house detective went out at a ponderous trot. The night-clerk stood trembling in an agony of fear.

"You're not the one who phoned down!" he said shrilly, to Traile. "You're not Mr. Greenwood."

Traile looked at the mummified figure on the bed.

"So that's why the door was locked," he muttered. "The poor youngster thought we were crooks."

The clerk backed away still farther, his watery eyes almost popping from their sockets.

"Good Lord!" he gasped. "You don't mean this—this is—"

Traile grimly nodded. The clerk turned a pasty white, whirled and fled from the suite. Eric followed Traile as the taller man went back beside the bed.

"Do you think it's really a plague?" he said tensely.

The bronzed secret agent shook his head.

"No, Eric, I'm afraid he is a victim of some deliberately planned horror."

"You mean Doctor Yen Sin?" exclaimed Eric.

"Yes, but don't ask me how it was done, or why." Traile's dark eyes shifted to the stand where the two highball glasses had stood. One was on the floor, and the other was in shattered fragments on the stand.

"Someone else was in here!" said Eric excitedly.

TRAILE LOOKED at the door. The night-latch was still locked. He glanced toward the open closet and into the bathroom. His face was taut, lined with anxiety.

"No one could've come in by the window," said Eric. "It's a hundred feet from the ground, and no fire-escape near it. I looked."

"I know," nodded Traile.

He turned soberly and leaned over the pitiful wreck which had only a few minutes before been a handsome youth. He took off Greenwood's coat and shirt, pulled up his undershirt. The

Traile wrenched at the gun
in the other's grasp.

mummified creature made no protest, seemed to be utterly unaware of anything. The uncanny song was still on his lips, but it had died to a plaintive moan.

From coat to undershirt, his clothes had a queer look of age and rottenness; they tore as Traile removed them. He bent down and scrutinized the shriveled body. It was dark, leathery, like the boy's face, but to a less degree. He touched the darkened skin. It felt dry, scorched, but the flesh beneath was firmer than he had expected.

Out in the night, a siren sounded with a muffled but slowly increasing volume. Traile raised his head.

"There's the ambulance. We'll soon have an expert opinion."

He stepped toward the window, then came back.

"Eric, maybe you'd better go down and be ready to meet the F.B.I. men. I'd like to have the senior agent see Greenwood before they move him."

Eric went out. Traile glanced compassionately at the strangely aged figure on the bed, then crossed to the luggage-stand to search Iris Vaughan's effects. The shriek of the ambulance siren grew louder, faded off with a final guttural note. And, as it ended, another and different sound came to his ears.

"Kill!" came a hoarse whisper from somewhere behind him. "Kill! Kill! Kill!"

Traile's eyes flicked up to the dresser mirror. Then he froze. Eyes wildly blazing, the mummified figure of Greenwood was stealing up behind him!

Just as he whirled, the mummy-man leaped for his throat. His unshriveled hand raked along Traile's jaw in a hasty but vain attempt to clutch him. Traile threw him off. Like a madman, he sprang back to the attack.

"Kill!" he snarled. "Kill! Kill!" Traile swung, but pity for that queerly demented creature took part of the force from his blow. The mummy-man staggered, plunged in like a human battering-ram. Traile tried to jump clear, struck the luggage-stand and tripped. Greenwood was on him in a flash, an animal-like cry bursting from his lips. Traile twisted as the mummy-man hurtled down upon him, and the snarling creature partly lost his grip.

Its shriveled hand clawed out toward Traile's eyes. Traile crashed his fist under the mummy-man's jaw. A broken whimper escaped the creature's lips, then it flung itself back into the fight.

"Kill—Kill!" it moaned. Its flaming eyes had lost all sanity.

Traile was on his knees. As the mummy-man charged, he seized one arm and spun around. Greenwood was jerked from the floor by the wrenching force of the trick. He went over Traile's head, struck almost flat on his back. Before he could move, Traile gripped the other arm and pinned him there, helpless.

The shock of his fall seemed to have partly stunned the mummy-man. He lay there panting, only the faintest whisper on his lips. He made no attempt to struggle further. Traile was cautiously releasing one arm, intending to secure Greenwood's belt and bind his hands behind him, when he heard the night-clerk's voice from the hall.

"In there. Please hurry. Get him out of here—"

TWO WHITE-CLAD interns, with a stretcher, appeared

in the connecting doorway. Back of them came the clerk. All three stared down at Traile and the mummy-man, faces amazed.

"He became violent," Traile explained tersely. "You'd better tie him to the stretcher. He might start in again."

The clerk gave a frightened little bleat and disappeared. The first intern stolidly opened his medicine kit and produced a hypodermic syringe.

"Just hold him that way a second more," he said to Traile. "This will take care of him till we get him to the hospital."

Traile turned Greenwood's right arm in position for the injection. The intern knelt, deftly inserted the needle.

"Now!" he said.

Too late, Traile caught the swift movement of the second intern. There came a sharp jab at the back of his neck. He lunged sidewise, briefly saw a second syringe as the other intern withdrew it from his neck. A thin, weasel face grinned down as he tried to get to his feet. Then his knees buckled, and he slid to the floor.

"Out cold!" he heard the second man mutter. "That stuff certainly works fast!"

Through the pounding agony in his brain, Traile heard a singsong voice speak from the doorway.

"Attend to the other one. There is no time to waste!"

He kept his eyes closed, setting his teeth against the frightful pain within his head. But for that childhood accident, he would have been senseless the moment he had fallen. Even now, his brain was throbbing a mighty protest at being driven to endure that hellish torture to which he should have succumbed.

"Hurry!" the singsong voice directed. "This changes our plans. Put the Q-Man on the stretcher—the other one will be taken down the rear way."

Traile felt himself lifted onto the stretcher. His arms and legs moved limply. Except for his head, his entire body was numb. He lay there, eyes closed, holding back a groan of agony by a mighty effort. He heard voices whispering, realized that more men had come into the room. Then a sheet was drawn over him, and the stretcher was hurriedly lifted.

He could tell they were taking him to the front elevators. He tried desperately to bring back the control of his numbed limbs, but they were devoid of feeling. The men with the stretcher moved at a fast trot, sending blasts of agony through his head at every step.

An elevator was waiting, and he heard the gasp of the operator as the men carried him into the cage. He tried to cry out, but no words came. The door closed and they dropped quickly. When they reached the lobby he heard the clerk's panicky voice.

"Oh, my God! Is he—"

"Yes, he's dead!" one of the stretcher-men said gruffly. "Better keep back—it's probably contagious."

The clerk moaned.

"This is awful! We'll be ruined. Wait! Take him out the side door. There's somebody coming—"

The stretcher jolted, and in a few moments Traile felt the cool night air as they emerged from the hotel. The breeze blew the sheet up at one corner, and by rolling his eyes sidewise he could see a little way. An ambulance stood in the driveway, and not far away he glimpsed a limousine in the shadows. Drivers stood by, and the engines of both machines were running. The rear door of the limousine abruptly swung open, but the sheet blew back in place before he could see any more. He heard soft footsteps.

"Move swiftly!" ordered a sibilant voice. "Federal agents will soon be here."

A cold perspiration broke out on Traile's forehead. It was the voice of Doctor Yen Sin!

"But, Master," whispered one of the men, "this is not—"

THERE CAME a sudden padding of feet on gravel. Traile heard the newcomer break into breathless speech. "Master! Five of Monsieur X's men—they have a machine gun. I saw them stealing this way!"

"*Allez!*" a man yelled from somewhere near-by. "This way—*vite!*"

Traile heard a swift scuffle, a howl of anguish. "Into the ambulance!" came the command of the Yellow Doctor. "Quick, fools!"

The stretcher was hurled into the car, and Traile heard someone climb in beside him. The sharp clatter of a machine gun echoed through the night. Someone screamed, then the ambulance leaped forward. Bullets thudded through the side of the car. Traile tensed as they zipped viciously above his head. The fusillade was over in a second, but it had done one thing.

His numbed body had started to function again. He could feel the nerves tingling in his arms and legs.

"Drive without lights!" the voice of Yen Sin commanded, directly above him. "Make all possible speed!"

"But the mummy-man, Master!" protested a frightened voice from up front. "He is back with the others."

"Have you lost your senses?" demanded the Crime Emperor. "He is here beside me."

"No, Master," exclaimed the other speaker, as the ambulance plunged on. "He was in the room, and our Group Control ordered us to take him. The mummy-man was to be carried down by the rear way."

Traile struggled fiercely to bring the strength back into his muscles, for he knew the revelation which was coming. The sheet was abruptly moved away from his face, and through barely opened eyes he saw Yen Sin bend over him in the gloom.

"A flashlight!" ordered the Yellow Doctor. "I shall soon know the reason for this."

Another man, farther back on the intern's seat beside the stretcher, bent over in the lurching ambulance. Traile closed his eyes an instant before the glow illumined his face.

Yen Sin drew in his breath with a hissing sound.

"It is Traile! We have succeeded at last."

"Tche!" said the man with the torch. "He will trouble us no more."

The Yellow Doctor laughed harshly.

"Finally, he sleeps! I was beginning to think the man had some occult power."

"Why not finish him at once, Master?" said the other man nervously.

"Where are your wits?" retorted Yen Sin contemptuously. "He possesses a secret enabling him to go for days without sleep. With that knowledge I shall be free to use the hours now wasted."

"But what of the mummy-man?" queried the one with the torch. "If he falls in the hands of those others, our work may be lost."

"Group Control has undoubtedly spirited him away in one of the escort cars," replied the Crime Emperor.

The light grew brighter through Traile's lids, and he surmised that Yen Sin had taken the torch and was leaning over him. Suddenly the man beside the Yellow Doctor gave a cry of alarm.

"The light, Master! We are followed!"

Almost in the same instant, the machine gun in the pursuing car chattered fiercely. The light went out, and the ambulance careened wildly around a corner. There was a rattle of shots from behind, and the bark of pistols mingled with the steadier pound of the machine gun.

"The escort must have caught up with them," exclaimed a voice from the driver's seat. "It's about time they—"

THE BRAKES squealed, and the ambulance went into a violent skid. The right side struck against something, and Traile was thrown halfway off the stretcher. Headlights cut through the darkness, as two cars came plunging around the corner. From where he lay, Traile saw the orange flash of pistol fire, then a tire blew out with a loud bang.

One pair of headlights swerved away as the crippled car mounted the sidewalk. The other machine jerked to a stop near the ambulance, and two men jumped out.

"Hurry, Master!" one of them cried in frantic Chinese. "The rest of the escort has been cut off!" The Yellow Doctor sprang from the ambulance. Two of his agents seized the end of the stretcher and started to transfer it. The machine gun in the other car cut loose with a murderous fire. Both of the men dropped. Splinters flew from the floor of the ambulance, and Traile felt the stretcher jump as a bullet clipped one handle.

He tried to get to his feet, but his half-numbed limbs refused to move. He had a fleeting glimpse of Doctor Yen Sin leaping into the escort car. Guns blasted again, then the escort machine rocketed away at a furious pace. From back in the direction of the Fairlawn, an exhaust whistle blew shrilly. Men poured from the car with the ruptured tire. The headlights were pointing away from the ambulance, but Traile could tell that they were white men. For an instant he thought they were police or F.B.I. agents. Then he heard a voice grate harshly in French.

"We must change to the ambulance!"

"But it's tangled with this other car," cried one of the men.

"*Cochon!* It will pull free if you back it hard enough! *Vite!* Those accursed Federal men will be here in a moment."

Two of the men gripped the stretcher handles, shoved vigorously. The sheet flapped back over Traile's face as they pushed him back into the ambulance. He heard the leader snap another command, and felt the car move as a man jumped into the driver's seat. Two others crowded into the rear as, with a final sharp order, the leader sprang in beside the driver.

The engine roared, and the ambulance bucked and tugged. Abruptly, it tore loose, with a scraping of broken fenders. In a second, it was hurtling down the street.

"Turn right, down the hill," Traile heard the leader say in muffled French. "The fog is thicker down there—we can lose them easier."

The exhaust whistle of the pursuing F.B.I. car steadily grew louder. Traile felt one of the men slide a machine gun along beside the stretcher.

"*Non, non!*" snapped the leader. "Shoot only as a last resort. We would have a hundred G-Men on our track by morning!"

The ambulance tilted in a reckless turn, plunged on downhill. Traile had made no effort to move since the gunmen climbed in beside him. Most of his strength had returned. The throbbing ache was gone from his brain, and, except for a pain at the back of his neck, he felt almost normal. But he knew the slightest move would bring an attack. He waited, grimly.

"Turn left," the mysterious leader ordered. Then, at some query Traile did not catch: "*Oui*, the same way."

The tires howled, and the ambulance lurched drunkenly. From the echoing roar of the engine, Traile guessed they were in an alley. The throb of the exhaust whistle began to fade out.

"Slower," snapped the man beside the driver. "We are safe now that—*Garde a vous!*"

The driver swore, slammed on the brakes. There was a terrific, jolting crash. One of the gunmen tumbled headlong onto Traile.

"Imbecile!" the leader said furiously. "Now, the whole pack will be after us!"

At his fierce command, the stretcher was lifted out. Traile heard broken glass and bottles rolling about, and surmised that the ambulance had struck a milk-truck. An angry shout, apparently from the truck driver, was cut short by the sound of a vicious blow. Traile heard the man fall, then someone hurried toward the stretcher.

"Take him down the usual way," the leader muttered. "Put him in the first room, then come back and guard the exit."

Traile stiffened for a leap from the stretcher. He was unarmed, but surprise would probably aid him to seize a gun or escape. Then he heard the scrape of the machine gun being drawn from the ambulance, realized the gunner was trotting along behind the stretcher. He swore under his breath. The gunman could mow him down before he was on his feet.

He relaxed his taut muscles. The leader had said something about leaving him in a room. Perhaps, then he would have a better chance for a break.

A door opened and shut, and in a moment he felt the slow downward motion of a freight elevator. It stopped, and there was a jingle of keys, then the click of a lock. The men roughly put down the stretcher. A faint glow shone through the sheet as a light was switched on. Then the door slammed.

Traile listened intently, trying to make sure there was no one else in the room. Not a sound broke the stillness. He carefully lifted one edge of the sheet.

He was lying near the center of a small, grimy storeroom, the type which could be found in almost any office building or apartment-house basement. A broken chair, some odd lengths of pipe, several striped canvas awnings ranged along one wall. At the other end of the room three lurid chromos had been tacked up, the center one under the dusty bracket-light which illuminated the room. There was no one in sight.

Traile threw back the sheet. He was halfway to his feet when he heard a low, grinding sound. He stared around, gave a start. The wall with the chromos was swinging inward like a huge door!

CHAPTER 7
SATAN'S SUBSTITUTE

TRAILE THREW himself back, hastily drawing the sheet over his face. As the hinged wall opened farther he heard the voices of two men. One he recognized at once as that of the mysterious leader, whom he knew must be "Monsieur X."

"The agents shot Mario," the other man said huskily. *"Mon Dieu, they just about cut him in two!"*

"Then he cannot talk," returned Monsieur X. "Here, help me carry our exhibit inside."

The stretcher was lifted, and Traile felt a current of warmer air as he was carried beyond the hinged wall. The men put him down, and he heard the wall swinging back into place.

"Go to the Cliff Hotel," said Monsieur X curtly, "and tell Rudermann we are ready. We will see what he has to say, before we deal with Hirati."

A door opened and shut with a soft thud. Traile heard a sound like a desk drawer being opened. That meant the man's attention would be temporarily diverted. He took a quick breath, and lunged to his feet.

Three yards away, a figure in black mask and robe whirled from behind a desk. On the front of his robe was a large letter X, in white. The mask covered his face clear to his lips.

As Traile leaped up, the man's mouth opened in amazement. Then, with frantic haste, he snatched at the gun before him. Traile's fingers were almost on the weapon when the masked man seized it and jumped back.

"Put up your hands!" he snarled in English.

Traile stood glaring into the eyes back of the mask slits, then slowly obeyed.

"So you knew, all the time!" grated the black-robed man. As Traile made no answer, he edged sidewise around the desk, keeping the gun leveled.

"Where is young Greenwood?" he demanded.

"Dead," said Traile grimly.

"You lie!" rasped the man in black. "I saw him—"

He jumped, as an electric bell on the side of the desk rang twice. For half a second, his gun was off its aim. Traile's long arm snaked downward. The masked man jerked the trigger, but

Traile's hand was already on his wrist. The bullet clipped the edge of the desk, made a crooked hole in the floor.

The roar of the pistol was like a small cannon in the closed room. Traile spun the other man around, expecting a charge of gunmen from the doorway. But no one appeared. The masked man swung venomously at Traile's jaw. Traile rolled with the blow, wrenched the gun from the other man's grasp.

Monsieur X whirled, then to Traile's amazement dived head-long at the wall on his right. A panel flew open, and the masked man disappeared in solid darkness beyond. Traile leaped after him. The panel had started to close, but it flew open again at his touch. The black-robed figure catapulted itself at him from the gloom. He lashed out, planted a left hook. The man grunted, came in again, clawing at the pistol.

Traile rammed the gun into his pocket, sprang past the somber figure. For just a moment, Monsieur X was outlined against the light from the other room. Traile shifted his weight and crashed an upper-cut to the masked man's jaw. Monsieur X toppled backward, pawed futilely at the air, and became a black heap on the floor. Traile hurriedly made certain the man was not shamming, then lit a match and looked about him.

THE ROOM was filled with cabinets and filing-cases. A safe stood in one corner. There was a steel-backed door made to slide in place behind the secret panel. If Monsieur X had had time to shove it in position, he would have been saved. The match burned out. Traile lighted another, bent over the uncon-scious man. Just then the electric bell in the next room rang shrilly.

From somewhere not far distant came the sound of excited voices. He dropped the match, wheeled and stared toward the other room. No one had entered, but the voices grew louder, and he knew it was a matter of seconds before someone would appear. He started to close the panel, then swiftly changed his mind. Stooping over, he stripped the mask and robe from that inert figure lying there in the dark.

A moment later, he stepped back into the other room. The black robe covered most of his clothes. He adjusted the mask, shot a quick glance sidewise to see that the swinging panel had closed.

He was taller than Monsieur X, but practice at impersonation had trained him to take inches from his height without great difficulty. He stepped away from the dim light, stole toward the door beyond which the voices had come. If only he knew how to open the hinged wall—

"Ah, *nom de Dieu!*" a man's voice suddenly screamed. The last word rose to a note of torture—and abruptly ended.

There followed a stark silence, a moment so still that it was more terrible than that tortured shriek had been. Traile reached under the black robe, took the automatic from his pocket.

Someone was approaching the doorway. He could not hear a sound, but he knew what was happening. Someone was stealing toward that door. He moved back to one side, where the shadows were blackest. With the robe and mask, he would be all but invisible.

The door began to move. Coolly, he lifted the gun. The shadow of a talonlike hand fell across the door. There was a long pause, then a yellow, Satanic face slowly came into view. Deliberately, Traile aimed the gun between the eyes of Yen Sin.

"Don't move, Doctor!" he said.

The tawny eyes flicked toward him. Somewhere behind Yen Sin, voices whispered tensely. But the Crime Emperor did not stir.

"Reach back and close the door," Traile said with a deadly coolness. "If it opens again—you die."

Doctor Yen Sin moved one yellow claw, and the door softly closed. As Traile took a step forward, the mandarin's thin lips curled in a mocking smile.

"For an amateur, Monsieur X, you do exceedingly well—or should I say '*Herr* X?'"

Traile eyed him silently through the mask slits.

"You see, *mein freund*," the Yellow Doctor went on in fluent German, "I have finally found who you are. You made a slight mistake tonight."

There was a rustling on the other side of the door. Traile calmly stepped in front of the Crime Emperor. Yen Sin spoke hurriedly in Chinese: "Await my word! He is in front of me, and you could not kill him now."

Traile smiled grimly back of the mask. But he spoke harshly, in French.

"You will talk only in the French tongue! I will have no Oriental trickery."

"You could learn much from it, *mein Herr* X," the Yellow Doctor said sardonically. "And now, if you will drop the pretense, perhaps we can arrange something to our mutual satisfaction."

TRAILE LOOKED at him over the gun. If he could carry on the role for a few minutes, he might learn the answer to the entire riddle. "I do not trust you, *Monsieur le Docteur*," he said coldly. "You have tried to have me murdered."

"And your machine gun was a toy, I suppose?" Yen Sin inquired in a silky voice. Then his tone hardened. "Since you prefer coarse tactics, I shall use them, also. Your motive is money alone—mine is power. You have certain information I desire. I have evidence which will hang you or place you before a firing squad."

Traile spoke with a calculated sneer.

"And you, Doctor, are facing a firing squad of one, with a small chance of escape."

"If you kill me," Doctor Yen Sin said calmly, "the men beyond that door will tear you to pieces. If you try to trick me, American military intelligence will have full information about you within twelve hours. And my agents will see to it that you do not escape from the city."

Traile glared at him through the mask slits.

"Well, then, what is it you wish?"

The Crime Emperor smiled thinly.

"You will learn, *Herr* X, that I do not wish—I command. You will tell me where you have hidden the man named Michael Traile. I know he is your prisoner, for you seized him by mistake."

"He escaped," Traile replied shortly.

"A lie," said Doctor Yen Sin. "But that we shall settle in a moment. You will also turn over to me the six books which were in the suitcase of Cyrus Greenwood, before you bribed the checkroom attendant to let you have them."

"Is that all?" Traile sneered.

"No," said the Crime Emperor slowly. "There is one other point. You will, tonight, become a member of the Invisible Empire, and turn over to me all the information you have stolen in these years."

"Do you think I am a fool?" Traile flung back in assumed rage. He stepped closer, with the gun almost at Yen Sin's heart. "What have you done with Paul Greenwood, you yellow fiend?"

The Crime Emperor's weird eyes drew into venomous slits.

"He is where you will never use him as you planned. And your so carefully guarded secret is in my hands!"

Traile could tell from Yen Sin's face that he expected an outburst.

"A clumsy trick to fool me!" he snarled.

A queerly startled light came in the Yellow Doctor's eyes. At first, Traile thought his words had caused it. Then he saw Yen Sin stare down at the bronzed hand which held the gun.

"Traile!" the Chinese whispered. For the first time since he had entered, a hint of fear came into his tawny eyes.

On the other side of the door, muttered voices sounded. Traile did not catch the words. Doctor Yen Sin partly turned his head as though to answer.

"Stand still," Traile ordered grimly. "From now on, I'll give all the orders."

The Crime Emperor faced him with a look of baffled hate.

"You will pay, Traile, for this night's work!"

"I'll risk that," the American retorted. "Get back against the door—and keep your hands spread sidewise!"

With a coldly furious glance, the Yellow Doctor obeyed. Traile watched closely, for he knew the folds of Yen Sin's mandarin robes might contain some deadly weapon, a search for which might be fatal in itself.

"Now," he said sternly. "What turned Tanati and Paul Greenwood into mummies?"

Doctor Yen Sin stood contemptuously silent. Traile slowly lifted the gun so that the Crime Emperor was looking straight into the muzzle.

"There are times," he said grimly, "when murder is not murder."

The contempt went out of Yen Sin's face. His eyes fixed themselves on Traile's, and the pupils suddenly expanded, growing as if by magic into black, evil pools. But the masked secret agent laughed shortly.

"Don't waste the effort, Doctor. I can't be hypnotized."

THE CRIME EMPEROR opened his lips for a snarled reply, but abruptly closed them again. At the same moment Traile heard the sound—a low tapping on the other side of the hinged wall. He stepped back, keeping Yen Sin covered. The sound grew louder, and then he saw the covert mockery in the Yellow Doctor's eyes.

"For a clever man, Mr. Traile, you are quite a fool. While you wasted this time, the rest of my men were finding the other entrance."

"They'll never save you," Traile said curtly.

He reached out, gripped Yen Sin's arm, forced the Crime Emperor across the room. They were near the secret panel when, with a low grinding sound, the hinged wall began to open.

The face of an Oriental appeared in the slowly widening space. The man gave a squeal as he saw Yen Sin, then vanished as though he had been pulled back by unseen hands. Suddenly, the snout of an automatic poked around the edge of the hinged wall. Traile fired, and the hand with the gun jerked out of sight. He heard a hasty whisper, and the light beyond the wall went out.

As Traile's shot roared, the door on the left burst open, and two of Yen Sin's men sprang into the room. Traile swung the Crime Emperor around to block their fire. The two Chinese leaped forward, and three more darted in through the doorway. Traile kicked back at the secret panel. His foot had barely touched it when a familiar voice yelped from the darkness beyond the now half-opened wall.

"Holy smoke—it's Doctor Yen Sin! Come on!"

Traile started. It was Eric Gordon!

In his surprise, he briefly relaxed his guard. The Yellow Doctor whirled, and, with a ripping of silken robes, was free. The five Chinese assassins had spun around in dismay, as Eric spoke. Yen Sin flung out a swift command and dived behind the desk. A group of armed men became visible beside the opened wall. Flame jetted from two guns, and one of Yen Sin's killers stumbled back in the entry through which he had come.

The Crime Emperor, shielded by the desk, was almost at the doorway. Two of the raiding agents jumped after him, and behind them Traile saw Eric and Major Locke. Forgetting his masked face, he sprang toward the first two men.

"Don't shoot! Take him alive!"

The first agent's gun was aimed straight at Yen Sin. Traile struck at his arm just as he fired. The bullet went through the door, high above Yen Sin's head.

Major Locke charged at Traile with an angry roar. Back of him came Eric and an Army captain. Traile's attempt to shout his identity was lost in the general uproar. The major's hand shot out and whisked the black mask away. His jaw sagged, and Eric halted, stunned, as he saw Traile's face.

"Save yourself, Traile!" came a sudden cry from Yen Sin.

The Crime Emperor sprang through the doorway, and two F.B.I. men dashed after him. Shots crashed from the other room as Yen Sin's men covered the escape of their master. The first agent jumped back. The other one leaped side-wise, his gun blazing toward the killers. Two more F.B.I. men ran in from the storeroom side, and a tommy-gun snarled into action.

Screams and groans from the other room told that the Federal men had done their work well. The agents plunged through, raced after Doctor Yen Sin, and in a few seconds the din had died away.

Locke and the Army captain, a young but shrewd-looking officer, had forced Traile back at gun point. Over Locke's shoulder, Traile saw Eric's dazed and incredulous face. As the tumult died out, Locke stepped back, carefully keeping Traile covered.

"Search him, Parker," he bluntly ordered the captain.

"I'm not the man you want," Traile said impatiently. "If you'll give me time to explain—"

"Shut up!" snapped the Intelligence major. "You made a fool of me before, but you won't do it again."

Eric pushed by Captain Parker.

"You're all wet on this!" he burst out. "He couldn't be Monsieur X."

Locke turned on him with a look of sudden suspicion.

"How do I know you're not in on this, too?"

Eric's fists clenched, but at Traile's quick glance he kept silent.

Captain Parker ran his hands over Traile's body, searched his pockets.

"He hasn't any other gun," he told Locke.

"Look here!" Traile rapped at the glowering major. "I can prove what I say in just a few seconds. The real Monsieur X is in another secret room connected with this one. I knocked him out when he tried to escape. And I took his mask and robe when I heard Yen Sin and his men coming."

Locke smiled sarcastically.

"And I suppose you can explain why you saved the Chinese from being shot and why he was so anxious for you to get away?"

Traile's dark eyes snapped.

"A child could see the answer to that," he retorted. "I wanted him alive, for questioning. As for the other, he saw a chance to implicate me in this affair, and discredit me so I'd be prevented from any further fight against the Invisible Empire."

"Fast thinking," sneered the major, "but it won't work."

Traile turned to the young captain, who was eying him uncertainly.

"If you'll push open that second panel, you'll find proof which may convince even your thick-headed senior."

Locke reddened angrily. While Captain Parker hesitated,

Eric shoved the panel open. He lit a match, and the flare illuminated the secret filing-room. Ignoring Major Locke's gun, Traile took a step toward the chamber. Then he halted in consternation.

Monsieur X had vanished!

CHAPTER 8
AT THE FOOT OF THE LADDER

FROM WHERE he stood in the opening, Traile stared around the room. Several file-cases had been hastily rifled, and the safe stood open. But there was no sign of an exit by which the spy could have escaped.

"Well," Major Locke said fiercely, "where's your man?"

"There must be a secret exit from the room," Traile answered.

"Which, of course, we won't be able to find," snorted Locke. He wheeled as two of the F.B.I. men hurried back into the room. "Did you catch that Chinese?"

"No," said one of the agents. "Two of his bodyguards stood us off long enough for him to get away."

Traile looked around. The agent who had answered was red-headed, and there was an efficient air about him.

"Is your name Dodd?" he asked.

The agent eyed him, nodded. "I'm the man who phoned you from the Fairlawn Hotel," said Traile. "I want you to put me under arrest." The red-headed agent looked as though he suddenly doubted his hearing. But Locke burst in before he could reply: "Be careful, Mr. Dodd! This man is dangerous—he's trying to trick you in some way."

Dodd scratched his thatch of red hair.

"Things have happened too fast for me," he said. He looked around the dim-lit underground office, then his candid eyes came back to Traile. "How can you prove you're whom you say you are?"

Traile extended his right index finger.

"There's ink on the desk—it will make a passable print."

Several more F.B.I. men had returned from the vain pursuit of Yen Sin. They watched curiously while Traile made the fingerprint. Dodd took an envelope from his pocket, removed a cardboard and compared the two prints. He glanced over at Locke.

"They're the same, all right," he said.

"That doesn't mean anything," grated the major. "It's exactly the same procedure he used to establish himself with us. It's obvious he's bamboozled some high-up official in the Government—tricked him into making him a secret agent so he could carry on with his crooked work."

"You're crazy!" Eric burst out indignantly. "He didn't even want to be tied up with the Government. I happen to know—"

"Never mind, Eric," Traile said quietly. "A long-distance call to Glover, or the State Department, will straighten things out."

Dodd looked dubiously from Traile to Major Locke.

"I'm still hazy about this," he said to the Intelligence officer. "Would you mind telling me where the Army fits in the picture?"

"It's partly confidential," said Locke. "If you'll tell me just how you stand on it, I'll explain all I can."

"Fair enough," said the red-headed agent. "I got a phone call about an hour ago, evidently from this man. He mentioned a special memo from Washington, which says we're to take orders from the man whose finger matches that print. He said to bring a squad to the Fairlawn. When we got there, this other chap"— he motioned to Eric—"took us up to see the 'Q' fellow and somebody he said had been hurt. The place was empty, and just then we heard a scrap down below.

"This young chap got excited and said they must have been kidnapped by Doctor Yen Sin. Our special memo also mentioned that name and some stuff on the Invisible Empire, so we chased downstairs. We had a three-sided fight with some Chinks and another outfit, then they all beat it. We chased them down-town—and you know the rest."

MAJOR LOCKE'S frosty blue eyes were fixed on Traile. He nodded doubtfully. "I understand a little more now—but the earlier affair is still a mystery." While Dodd and his agents listened in amazement, he described the incident of Tanati and the mummy-case, then what had followed.

"The whole thing seems inextricably tangled up," he said. "I'm positive that this Q-Man is Monsieur X, the free-lance spy who has given us so much trouble. Those files in there undoubtedly contain confidential Army and Navy plans and information he has stolen. I'll have them removed to headquarters to check up. But this other things—I can't understand it."

"It's the craziest thing I ever heard of," agreed Dodd. "What happened after you left that place? Did you catch Meredith?"

"No, he got away. And I couldn't find Flaherty so I took a taxi and went to the Fairlawn, knowing that this Q-Man had gone there. I arrived there just about the end of the fight. I hear a man shouting in French, and I immediately thought of Monsieur X. I followed in the taxi, but my driver refused to keep up with the ambulance. Then a car passed with an exhaust whistle blowing—it must have been yours—and we managed to follow it to this building."

The red-headed F.B.I. man glanced at Parker.

"Was the captain with you all this time?" he asked Locke.

"No," said the major, "he was keeping track of a man named Rudermann, whom we believe to be a German foreign agent. He just told me a few minutes ago that Rudermann had come to one of the offices in this building, about twelve-thirty tonight. He didn't see him go out, and he was still trying to find what had happened to him when all this occurred."

"The German must've gone out this way," ventured one of the agents, pointing past the hinged wall. "The other entrance is through a small office, at the rear of the first floor. That's how that Chinese escaped—by the office."

Traile had kept calmly silent while Locke and Agent Dodd were talking. Now, he turned to Captain Parker.

"Who was the Chinese," he inquired coolly, "whom I saw just as the wall swung back?"

"We found him tapping the wall when we searched the basement," Parker replied tersely.

"Where is he now?" said Traile.

Parker looked annoyed, went into the storeroom and switched on the light. The sprawled figure of an Oriental lay on the dusty floor.

"There he is. I knocked him out when he yelled as the wall was opening."

"Then he opened it?" Traile asked.

"No, it was—" Parker stopped, shrugged his immaculate shoulders. "We were all pressing close around, after we got the idea that there was a secret opening. I don't know who touched the release."

"All this is getting us nowhere," snapped Locke. He turned to Dodd. "Army Intelligence has been looking for Monsieur X for several years. This Q-3 business is plainly a cover-up for his spying activities."

"Q-3?" exclaimed Dodd. "He's called 'Q-5' in our special memo."

"That settles it," growled the major. "He's pulled the wool over the eyes of those dumb bureaucrats in Washington. All the time he's been stealing our secrets and working hand in hand with this Chinese criminal while pretending to be fighting him. But he's through now. I'll have him locked up and in irons within thirty minutes."

Eric Gordon shot a desperate look at Traile.

"Michael! You know you can prove it's all wrong!"

Traile's deep-tanned face lit with a sad smile.

"You go along with Dodd, old man, and report to Glover

through him. Perhaps it's wiser for me to let the Army investigate my part in this."

Major Locke beckoned to Parker.

"Take charge of the prisoner, Captain."

Traile's shoulders drooped wearily, as Parker came forward. The officer halted with military smartness, made a curt gesture with his pistol for Traile to precede him. Traile took a lagging step—then his hand shot out with lightning speed.

In a split second, Parker's gun was in his hand. He leaped backward toward the secret panel. One of the F.B.I. men snatched out his automatic. Traile took swift aim and fired. The agent's weapon struck the floor, shot cleanly from his hand.

Locke's pistol blasted, and the bullet clipped Traile's sleeve. Before he could fire again, Traile hurled himself into the secret room. The steel-backed barrier slammed into place under his swift-moving fingers.

BULLETS THUDDED through the wood, clanged dully against the steel. Traile jumped to his feet, hastily lit a match. He found a switch, turned on the lights, and wheeled for a quick survey. Outside, a fierce clamor was raging. Locke's harsh voice rose above the rest.

"Use the tommy-gun! That ought to batter it down!"

Traile cast a glance at the floor. No sign of a trapdoor there. The ceiling also looked solid. He ran to the nearest cabinet. The door was locked. He tried the next.

The steel barrier trembled under a burst from the sub-machine gun. Traile groaned. They would break through in a minute, and his quickly thought-out scheme would be lost. Even Eric, now, might believe him guilty.

His dark eyes suddenly gleamed. Two faint marks showed in front of the fourth filing-case, like tracks of small, flat wheels. He snatched at the case, pulled hard. It moved, rolled away from the wall, disclosing a space a foot wide and about four feet high. There was a heavy-spring device to pull it back into place.

The steel door was jumping under another blast from the tommy-gun. Traile squeezed through the narrow aperture. The tunnel beyond was wider, but he still had to stoop. He had a moment when he could see where it had been crudely boarded, then the filing-case rolled back against the hole and left him in total darkness.

He lighted another match, saw that he had only two left in the packet. Behind him, the machine gun gave a last short clatter and was silent. He moved ahead as fast as he could without blowing out the match. The passage turned and he saw a wooden door, studded with rusty bolt-heads. It, too, had a powerful spring. He twisted a long iron handle, and the door ponderously squeaked open. As he passed through, he saw the reason for the scores of bolts.

The other side was cleverly faced with sections of old bricks. The bolts were sunk into lead sockets in the bricks and they did not show.

The spring hauled the door shut, and the edges were instantly hidden. His match burned out. The next one flared and died, but in the brief interval he saw that he had emerged in an old gas-pipe conduit, apparently now unused. Lighting the last match, he hurriedly looked about him. There was an iron-runged ladder about forty feet away. As he neared it, he saw a man-hole cover at the top. He was about to climb up when his gaze fell on something near the foot of the ladder.

It was an old book.

He hastily picked it up. The sudden motion put out the match. He thrust the book under his coat, went up the ladder. Distant street sounds were vaguely audible through the manhole cover. Cautiously, he pushed up the heavy lid, then shoved it aside and climbed out.

He stood in a dark alley, one end cut off by a building so that it formed a cul-de-sac. Without stopping to replace the cover, he ran at top speed for the open end of the alley, where streetlights made a blur in the fog.

Ten minutes later, he stopped beside the taxi which Eric and he had parked on the edge of Chinatown. No one was near, and the shadows hid him as he unlocked the door. Something dropped to the floor when he bent over the kit in the rear of the car. He pulled down the special curtains, switched on a light at the back of the front seat.

The book he had found lay at his feet. He snatched it up, opened it to the flyleaf. Written there in an eccentric scrawl was the name, Cyrus Greenwood. An eager light came into Traile's dark eyes.

Hastily, he riffled the pages, then more carefully. But there was nothing hidden between them. For a moment he stared blankly at the title.

"Well, I'll be damned," he muttered. *"A Bicycle Trip Through Holland!"*

CHAPTER 9
WEB OF THE
INVISIBLE EMPIRE

NEAR THE center of the miniature city, a blue light suddenly glowed in a tiny building. Doctor Yen Sin leaned forward, and a long finger touched a button. "Control, Group D," an uneasy voice spoke from the hidden amplifier.

"Report on the search for Michael Traile," ordered the Yellow Doctor coldly.

"Still no word," came the answer, with a hint of desperation. "We are covering every point where he might—"

"Thirty-five hours have passed since he disappeared," interrupted the Crime Emperor. "The man must be found!"

"I believe he must have been killed, Master," protested the unseen spy. "Or else he has fled the city, to escape the authorities who are also searching for him."

The Yellow Doctor's eyes slitted with repressed anger.

"He is here in San Francisco, working to find evidence to clear himself. There are certain focal points he is bound to be watching. Double your group force and note everyone who comes near these spots."

"Yes, Master," said the spy hastily.

The blue light went out. Doctor Yen Sin switched to a different circuit, but no light flickered in the tiny city.

"Condensed report on Eric Gordon," he directed, without waiting for a reply to the signal.

"Connecting with previous report," said a singsong voice. "At noon, left offices of Federal Bureau of Investigation, Post Office Building, in company Special Agent Dodd and three other agents. To luncheon at St. Francis Hotel, returned one thirty-eight. At three-five went with Agent Dodd to conference with Major Locke at Presidio. Departed four-nineteen. Returned to Bureau offices, and still there at time of last report, seven-ten."

"Order all exits watched," ordered the Crime Emperor. "Other reports indicate they are planning a coup."

"The men are placed, Master," the singsong voice answered. "But I have another report. Monsieur X has just arrived, and is awaiting your pleasure."

"You will discontinue the use of his assumed title," said Yen Sin curtly. "From now on, he will be known merely as 'Agent N-33.'"

"*Tche*, Master," said the other man submissively.

"Have him brought to the audience cell," commanded the Yellow Doctor. "Receive all reports until further orders."

It was hardly half a minute when a buzzer gave a low-pitched signal and a bright red light went on at the farther end of the room. Doctor Yen Sin spoke a brief order toward the concealed microphone, and two sections of tapestry moved back with a rustling sound. At the same time, the red light went out and a spotlight shone down on the man who appeared there. He stood behind a door made entirely of glass, and the brilliant glare revealed that he was inside a cubicle so narrow that only a child could have squeezed into it with him. His head was covered with a loose gray hood which had no openings for eyes or mouth.

"Number?" said the Yellow Doctor tonelessly.

"N-33," the man replied in a hoarse voice. "I—I came about the sixth book."

Yen Sin's tawny eyes narrowed.

"You were given twelve more hours. The time is almost up."

"But, my God, I tell you I lost it!" moaned the man in the glass-fronted cell. "I've looked—"

"Failure in the Invisible Empire is severely punished," Yen Sin said without emotion. "It is now forty minutes past seven. You have until ten o'clock."

"Then give me someone to help," pleaded the man in the cell. "There's only one thing I can think of. If I could find that man, Traile—"

The Yellow Doctor started.

"What connection has he with the sixth book?" he demanded.

"Maybe not any," said the other man miserably. "But the conduit is the only place I can think where I might have dropped it. He escaped through there—"

"Fool!" said the Crime Emperor. "Why didn't you tell me this before?"

"I didn't think of it until tonight," replied the wretch in the cell. "But even if he did find it, he couldn't learn the secret without the other books."

"One hint might be enough," responded Doctor Yen Sin. "It is doubly important to find that book now."

IN THE pause which followed, the heavy breathing of the hooded man could be heard through the amplifier connected with the cubicle. The Yellow Doctor slowly interlaced his sharp-nailed fingers.

"Listen closely," he commanded. He spoke in rapid English for two minutes. As he concluded, the hooded man nodded.

"I understand," he mumbled.

"Before you go," said the Crime Emperor, "let me remind you of the—ceremonies—attending your entrance into the Empire last night."

"I haven't forgotten," the man groaned.

"Also, keep in mind the evidence which has been collected in the past forty-eight hours," Yen Sin added with a note of menace. "The War Department would be greatly interested in your private record, especially for the periods of the world war and the last three years."

Perspiration had soaked through the gray hood, where it touched the other man's forehead. He made an attempt to answer, but it was only a croaking sound. The Yellow Doctor smiled, spoke in Chinese. The spotlight went out, and the divided tapestries rustled back to cover the thick glass door.

The room with the miniature city remained in darkness. For a long time Doctor Yen Sin sat there, so still that, to anyone listening, the chamber would have seemed empty. The lights in the tiny buildings remained unlit, as the minutes passed. Half an hour went by—an hour—

The muffled buzzer sounded, and the Crime Emperor lifted his head. "Report," he said in a tired voice. "We have found the Q-Station, Master!" came the tense answer. Doctor Yen Sin swiftly sat up. "Details!" he commanded.

"Eric Gordon and Agent Dodd left Post Office Building at eight fifty-five, by a rear door. They met Major Locke and took a taxicab. They changed cabs twice to throw off pursuit, but Observer 96 followed. They left the third cab in the Latin Quarter, proceeded on foot to small apartment building known as the Laconia. It is on Kearny Street, near Telegraph Hill. Not known which apartment being used. Two on top floor, facing south, have shuttered windows, and three on other floors. Observer 96 relaying reports by drug-store phone on corner. Group D surrounding the area."

"Connect Observer 96," the Yellow Doctor ordered.

The hidden amplifier clicked.

"Main Control," Doctor Yen Sin said in mandarin dialect.

"Control, Group D, replacing Observer 96," a low voice replied with instant deference.

"Full reports," ordered Yen Sin, "but avoid arousing suspicion of those in the drugstore."

"There has been a peculiar incident, Master," came a whisper from the amplifier. "We are not the only ones watching Gordon and the others. Female Agent 85 just encountered Captain Parker acting in a suspicious manner, in car parked half a block from the apartment. She said he was bending over to avoid being seen. She also reports there are other men concealed in the rear of the car."

"Keep them under observation," directed Yen Sin.

"I have already ordered it. But here is a new report, from Observer 96."

"Let him make it personally," interrupted the Crime Emperor. There was a moment's delay, then the other spy spoke in a panting voice.

"Master, I have just seen Colonel Manning enter the building. He climbed the fire-escape at the rear, and went in through a hall window."

Yen Sin's hand moved swiftly toward one of the buttons recessed in the table.

"Are you sure of his identity?" he demanded of the observer.

"I am positive, Master. He was wearing civilian clothing, but it was the face of the American colonel. I saw his gray hair, and he limped as the Colonel limps."

A green bulb winked from the miniature Presidio. Doctor Yen Sin bent forward.

"Observer 96, instruct your Group Control to stand by." He connected the other circuit. "Are you certain of earlier report on the movements of Colonel Manning?"

"I made sure of it myself," came the prompt answer.

A triumphant gleam shone in Yen Sin's eyes. He switched back to the other line, gave concise instructions in Chinese. As the amplifier clicked into silence, he stood up and turned on the serpent-shaped lights. His weird eyes slanted back toward the miniature city, glanced from a pagoda-roofed building to one partly up the slope of Telegraph Hill. His yellow face held a mirthless smile as he turned to leave the room.

CHAPTER 10
THE FACE AT THE WINDOW

MAJOR LOCKE said shortly: "But what's the idea of this place?" He waited for an answer. Eric Gordon hesitated, glancing around the apartment which Traile and he had fitted up as the San Francisco Q-Station.

"It's supposed to be confidential," he muttered, "but those messages from Washington change everything. There's a secret base like this in every city where the Invisible Empire is suspected of operating. As I told Dodd, the switchboard in that closet has direct wires to Washington and New York, beside the lines to the Bureau, Presidio, Mare Island Navy Yard, and three or four other contact points near here. There is also a special radio and an emergency transmitter."

"A fine set-up," said Locke disagreeably. "No wonder this fellow Traile has been able to get away with murder."

Eric jerked around, his blue eyes blazing.

"One more crack about him, and I'll bust you right in the mouth!"

"For an innocent man," sneered Locke, "you're damned quick to defend him."

Eric lunged at him, but Agent Dodd hurriedly separated them.

"Cool down, you two! We're here on official business. If you want to scrap—wait till this thing's settled."

Major Locke sat down, staring sullenly at Eric. Dodd looked at his watch.

"Nine-thirty. Have you got those lines plugged in, Gordon?"

Eric nodded glumly. Dodd glanced at the steel-shuttered windows.

"You must have been expecting trouble, all right."

Eric managed a crooked grin.

"Well, we got it, didn't we?"

"If you ask me," Major Locke growled, "the whole thing is insane. That mummy business, to start with. Then Meredith disappears, and we find out his daughter was kidnapped. Then they both come back and swear they can't remember anything that happened during those twenty-four hours."

"The police surgeon told me it was true amnesia," interrupted Dodd. "Those hours are just a blank to them."

Eric stopped abruptly in the act of filling his pipe.

"Say, maybe they were hypnotized! Michael told me that Yen Sin could hypnotize people so that they'd forget everything— or else do something he wanted, a long time after he put them to sleep."

Dodd wagged his head.

"Post-hypnotic suggestion. That explains how the yellow devil keeps people in hand, I guess. That and the torture stuff you told me about."

"I wonder what ever happened to Flaherty?" Lock said abruptly.

"Probably the Pole killed him and hid his body," said the red-headed agent. "There certainly were some queer things that night. Young Greenwood snatched after that mummy affair, and no sign of him; that Jap committing hari-kari—the cops proved he was the one that was seen running away from the fight. I think he was bumped off, instead of killing himself, because he'd seen too much. But I still can't figure why Traile wanted me to put him under arrest."

"I can," Eric asserted, with an angry look at Major Locke. "He knew he wouldn't be tied up with a lot of Army red tape. He'd have called Director Glover and got things straight in no time."

"Speaking of Glover," said Dodd, "it's funny that his call doesn't come through." He turned to Locke. "What time did that War Department message say your call would be?"

"I don't know," replied Locke, frowning. "I didn't actually see the message. Colonel Manning told me about it when I called the Presidio about an hour ago. He told me to meet you at once, that the Department was going to send an important message they didn't want sent over our regular wires. I supposed it was coming through your Bureau, until you brought me to this place."

"Well, something must be up," said Dodd.

ERIC PUFFED at his briar a moment, then went into the closet. None of the signal lights on the switchboard were lit. He was bending over the radio when there came a muffled tap at the door. He whirled, reaching for the gun he had placed on the table. Dodd and the Major had jumped up. Eric put out the lights, lifted his gun and jerked the door open. The silver-haired old man, who stood there, stepped back in alarm as he saw Eric's automatic. Locke gave an exclamation of surprise.

"Colonel Manning! I didn't expect you—"

"Not so loud!" said the other man, in an undertone. He peered down the hall, then limped into the room, tightly holding a brief-case.

Eric turned on the lights, laid down his gun.

"Beg your pardon, Colonel," he said, embarrassed, "but I was afraid it might be—"

"No apology needed," said the older man. He had limped over to the windows, was squinting down the shutters. "Turn off all but that table lamp," he whispered. "I came through the alley, and I could see this place was occupied."

Eric complied, somewhat puzzled and uneasy at the colonel's manner. The old man seemed to sense his feeling. He beckoned to Locke.

"Explain who I am, Major."

"This is Colonel Manning, Chief of Corps Area Intelligence," Locke said. He introduced Eric and Dodd. A brief smile touched Manning's kindly face as he inclined his head, then it shadowed with its former careworn look.

"Sit down, gentlemen," he said gravely. "I shall explain why I am here, in a moment." Then he turned to Locke. "Have you ever entertained any suspicion of Captain Parker?"

Locke's bristling eyebrows went up in a look of amazement.

"Parker! Good Heavens, sir—no, I never even considered—"

"I asked," said the gray-haired officer, "because he tried to follow me here tonight. I managed to give him the slip by coming through the alley."

"But what on earth—" Locke broke off, with a stunned expression. "You surely don't suspect he could have some connection with Traile—Monsieur X?"

The other man stared down at the West Point ring on his blue-veined hand. His face was in the shadow of the lamp.

"I'm afraid it is more than suspicion," he said slowly. "But we'll come to that later. I have been given an important task, and each of you will have to play a part in it."

He seated himself, a little wearily, and drew a sealed envelope from the briefcase. As he broke the seal he peered across the table at Eric and Dodd.

"This letter was delivered to me by an Army pilot, who flew here today from Washington. With it were full instructions for meeting you here, with Major Locke. The earlier messages, referring to secret orders tonight, were intended only to assemble us here."

He unfolded the enclosed sheets. Eric Gordon gave an exclamation.

"That's Michael's writing! He's reached Washington and squared everything!"

DODD AND Major Locke stared at the letter. The gray-haired officer began to read in a slow, precise voice. All were silent as he read:

"To Colonel Manning:

"In order to follow out the operation plan at the end of this message, there are a few salient points you should know. Eric Gordon will be able to explain the details as you require them. "There is, hidden somewhere in San Francisco, a dangerous Chinese criminal known as Doctor Yen Sin. The plan attached is intended to destroy him and his Invisible Empire. The mysterious events on the night of September eleventh were apparently caused by a struggle between Doctor Yen Sin and a man known as 'Monsieur X,' over the possession of a secret means for mass murder. I believe the secret was originally possessed by Cyrus W. Greenwood, research scientist for the Army during the world war. "This dangerous secret is probably now in the hands of Yen Sin, after his forcing Monsieur X into his Empire. The shortest means of learning Yen Sin's whereabouts will be to force the information from this man who has posed as a French free-lance spy. This should be simple, as the man is an officer in the United States Army. He was commissioned during the war when his German-American parentage was minimized, after certain apparent acts of bravery. Pretending to serve America, he secretly was on the rolls of German Intelligence. Since the war, he has sold military information to foreign countries. He is stationed at the Presidio and his name—"

With an oath, Locke jumped to his feet. A gun seemed to leap from nowhere into his fingers. The colonel's blue-veined hand shot out and gripped Locke's wrist. The major gave a howl of pain, and the pistol dropped to the floor. He hurled himself furiously at the frail-looking man before him. There was a crunching sound as a blue-veined fist thudded under Locke's jaw. He staggered back against the wall, dazedly slid to the floor and sat there.

"Cover him, Eric," said the colonel, in a suddenly crisp voice.

Eric's mouth popped open.

"Michael!" he gasped. "How in—"

Traile smiled grimly through his makeup.

"Explanations later. Let's get Monsieur X on his feet. I've a few questions to ask him."

Locke winced as Traile gripped his shoulder and hauled him up. His stunned expression quickly changed, and he jerked around to Dodd with some of his old fierceness.

"This is a damned frame-up! I suddenly realized he wasn't Colonel Manning—that's why I pulled the gun."

Traile reached out toward Locke's back and pulled his coat down from his shoulders, so that the major's arms were pinioned. While Eric covered the fuming officer, he took a knife from his pocket and slit Locke's shirt.

"Look at this," he said to Eric and Dodd.

A bandage pad had slipped down, and there, on Locke's shoulder, partly hidden by his undershirt, was an ugly brand in the shape of a coiled cobra.

"Good Lord!" said Dodd. "What's it mean?"

Traile answered: "My guess was right. The Doctor forced him to join the Invisible Empire."

Fear and rage alternated in the prisoner's face.

"You framed this whole thing," he snarled at Traile. His venomous eyes darted toward Dodd. "Are you going to let him get away with that—impersonating an Army officer, sending false messages—"

"Save your breath, Locke," Traile said coolly. "This time I'm on sure ground."

He turned to Dodd.

"Director Glover is waiting on our direct Washington line. Plug in the socket marked *D. J. 1*, and he'll O.K. me."

DODD HURRIED in to the switchboard.

Traile took a small make-up kit from the brief-case, set to work while Eric guarded the prisoner. "I'll give you your choice, Locke," he said calmly. "Lead us to Yen Sin's base—or hang."

"You can't bluff me," said Locke thickly, but his face was a leaden color.

Traile rubbed an alcohol solution over his hands, critically watched the blue-veined skin change to its normal bronze.

"That milk-truck driver died," he observed casually. "It was in tonight's paper. Since I was an eyewitness—"

"You couldn't have seen it," Locke blurted out. "Your face was covered—"

"The sheet was up at one corner," Traile lied coolly. "I saw the whole thing."

A sickly fear came into the traitor's eyes. Traile removed his gray wig, pretended not to notice.

"You'll hang for that alone," he said, "unless I persuade Washington that you might trade some espionage secrets in return for a prison term."

"What do you want me to do?" asked Locke hoarsely.

"Lead a raiding party to Yen Sin's hide-out," said Traile.

Locke shuddered.

"He'd burn me alive! I saw proof of that last night."

Traile heard Dodd's lowered voice as the agent talked with Glover. In a minute, Dodd came out. There was a new respect in his eyes as he looked at Traile.

113

"Sorry things got mixed up, sir. The chief certainly put me straight."

"Well, that's more than I am," said Eric. "I'm still in a fog about Tanati and Paul Greenwood."

Traile had finished removing the makeup from his face. He turned grimly to Locke.

"I was coming to that matter. I know the trick Yen Sin pulled on you with Tanati and the mummy—but where is the thing hidden now?"

"I don't know," Locke mumbled. "He stole it that night—"

"And the books?" Traile shot at him.

"Yes, he made me—"

From out in the hall came a stifled cry. Then someone beat desperately upon the panels of the door.

"Eric!" a girl's voice moaned. "Eric—open the door!"

"It's Sonya!" Eric shouted. He sprang before Traile could stop him.

In a wild leap, Major Locke was at the window and flung the shutters open, was halfway out when Dodd dragged him back. Locke savagely pulled away and dashed for the adjoining room, the agent at his heels.

Traile had seized Locke's gun as Eric threw open the door. He had a quick glimpse of Sonya Damitri, her dark eyes wide with a strange light.

"Eric!" she whispered. She took a step inside, then stood as though turned to stone. Even in that moment, with the spy and Dodd struggling fiercely in the next room, Traile felt a shiver go over him at the eerie look in her eyes.

"Sonya! What is it?" he heard Eric cry out as he whirled to help Dodd.

She gave a strangled sob, but the sound was lost in a high, queer wailing. Traile jerked back, his blood suddenly cold. It was the weird, wordless chant he had heard from the lips of Paul Greenwood!

As he turned, the wailing rose to a shrill and piercing note, so shrill it seemed his ears would burst Then it ended, and an odd, flickering glow began to shine at the window. In amazement he watched it, oblivious to the startled cry which had burst from Sonya's lips.

The light brightened, became a glowing circle which spread across the open space and shone into the room. Something moved in the center, grew into grim outlines. Traile went rigid.

Staring out of the light was the face of Doctor Yen Sin!

CHAPTER 11
CHINATOWN S.O.S.

FOR AN instant, as Traile saw the face of the Yellow Doctor, he thought Yen Sin had somehow reached the window. Then, with a start, he realized that it was an image projected into the light. But the Doctor's lips were moving, and his sibilant voice was audible there in the room!

"Use caution!" it whispered. "I wish them only to be stunned."

Agent Dodd had overcome Locke and shoved him back toward the first room. The spy gave a shriek of terror as he saw Yen Sin's face, and, with a sudden maniacal strength, broke away again. As Dodd raced after him, Eric sprang toward the window, lifting his automatic.

"Get back!" Traile shouted. He leaped after the other man. Eric's gun was already blazing at the face framed there in the light. But only a gloating smile curled the Yellow Doctor's lips.

"Be quick!" his voice came out of the light. "But be sure you make no mistake." Traile seized Eric, pulled him away from the window. Something near his elbow gleamed in the light as he turned. He dropped Eric's arm and jumped toward Sonya. In her hand was a small, pearl-handled pistol. It was pointed at Eric's back, and her finger was slowly tightening on the trigger.

"Look out, Eric!" Traile cried. He snatched at the pearl-handled gun. His fingers grazed Sonya's arm, just as Eric whirled. Flame streaked from the pistol, but his frantic leap had been in time. The bullet struck the wall.

Traile tore the weapon from the girl's unresisting fingers. The weird light shone on her beautiful face, and he saw it was ashen-white. Slowly, the dazed stare went out of her eyes and she took a stumbling step forward.

"Eric!" she said brokenly. "Oh, God—I almost killed you!"

Then, with a sob, she turned and ran into the hall.

"Wait!" Eric burst out. "Sonya—wait!"

Traile caught at him, but Eric threw him off and dashed after her. Traile started in pursuit, then remembered Dodd and the major. He wheeled, keeping out of the uncanny light as much as he could. Yen Sin's malignant features were still visible, but his head was now turned side-wise. Suddenly, a look of suspicion crossed that evil face. His voice echoed furiously in the Q-Station room.

"What have you done? You are using the visible light!"

Another face—the face of a frightened old man—abruptly appeared in the mysterious circle of light. His lips moved in a wild cry which drowned the voice of Yen Sin.

"Help!" he screamed. "Send police to Chinatown—to the pagoda building at—"

The yellow talons of the Crime Emperor flashed toward his throat, and his words ended in a gasp. Both faces now blurred, like a moving-picture film out of focus, then the glowing circle vanished. Only the lights of San Francisco, as seen from the slope of the hill, remained visible through the window.

Traile ran into the next room. Another shuttered window had been opened, and, as he reached it, he saw Dodd run along the fire-escape platform a floor below. Locke was darting down the iron ladder, with the F.B.I. man close behind. Traile raced back and into the hall. Several apartment dwellers gaped at him as he ran down the stairs.

A FIGHT was raging outside the building. He heard shots and yells, then the roar of cars speeding away. When he reached the front entrance, he saw Dodd emptying his gun at a machine which was whirling down the hill. Two Chinese and a uniformed soldier lay dead in the street, and a third Oriental was retching out his life with a bullet-hole in his stomach. Captain Parker jumped from a car across the street, as Traile hurriedly appeared.

"Right here, sir!" he called excitedly.

Traile shouted at Dodd, and the F.B.I. man dashed after him.

117

There in the entry was glaring Malay, a blowgun in his lips.

As they tumbled into the rear of the car, Parker let out the clutch. The machine hurtled down the slope at a reckless speed.

"What happened to Eric?" Traile fired at the Army officer.

"They seized him when he ran out after the girl," Parker said tensely. "My men tried to save him, but they were afraid to use the machine gun for fear of hitting Gordon."

Traile's jaw set tautly.

"We'll have to catch that car! If he falls into Yen Sin's hands, he'll die a horrible death!"

"They're in the car ahead of that," cut in Dodd. "Locke's in that one—the rat!"

Captain Parker was crouched over the wheel, and the car rocketed through the Quarter.

"My other squad is trying to follow them!" he tossed back through strident blasts of his horn. "But it took us off guard, the way this happened."

"My scheme went wrong," Traile said grimly. "Locke would have broken and talked in a few more minutes. But Sonya, and that business at the window, ruined everything."

"What the devil was that?" exclaimed Dodd. "I didn't have much chance to see, fighting with Locke."

"It was an attempt of Yen Sin's to make us helpless so we could be easily captured," said Traile. He stared at the fleeing car. "Thanks to one man's courage, it didn't succeed."

"You mean Eric Gordon?" asked Dodd. "No, though he's brave enough. But he thought it was really Yen Sin at the window. I meant Cyrus Greenwood."

Parker threw a hasty question over his shoulder.

"I don't get all this. What happened?"

Traile told him, swiftly, while the Army machine weaved and dodged through increasing traffic.

"Sonya must have been with the spies, watching the place," he added. "She was trying to warn Eric that he was in danger."

"But you just said she tried to kill him," exclaimed Parker.

"She didn't know what she was doing," Traile told him. "Doctor Yen Sin evidently had hypnotized her sometime before. Probably he planted a post-hypnotic command that the next time she tried to save Eric she would kill him. She came into the place to warn him—then the delayed hypnosis took effect. Temporarily, her conscious mind was a blank."

Dodd gripped the side of the car, as Parker made a reckless turn.

"But I heard that Chinese devil's voice, telling her what to do," he objected.

"That's what I thought, at first," said Traile. "Then I saw the glassy look in her eyes and I knew the truth. Yen Sin wasn't talking to anyone in that room. And he didn't intend for her to be there. He didn't even know we could see his face. All that was an attempt by poor old Cyrus Greenwood to direct the police to the Doctor's base. I'm afraid he'll pay for it with his life."

A HUGE bus suddenly appeared in their path, as they reached Columbus Avenue. Parker threw on the brakes, swearing vigorously. The bus halted for several seconds. By the time they could proceed, the car they had been chasing was lost from sight.

"Go on to Stockton—then down Sacramento!" Traile rapped

out. "Our only chance now is to beat Locke to the place he's undoubtedly making for."

"Then you know where it is?" Dodd queried eagerly.

"Only the alleyway that leads to it," Traile said, as the car leaped forward again. "I followed Locke last night, knowing he was Monsieur X, and that Yen Sin had discovered the fact, too. I knew the Doctor intended to force him to become a member of the Invisible Empire, so he could make use of Locke's assignment to Army Intelligence and also to take over all the foreign espionage information Locke had. But I did a poor job of shadowing, and Locke gave me the slip at the last moment."

Parker slowed briefly for a red light, then sent the car speeding through the intersection.

"It handed me a jolt when you gave me the proof about Locke today," he said to Traile.

"My 'proof' was half guesswork," Traile said dryly. "That's why I insisted on not telling Colonel Manning. He'd have arrested Locke and ordered a regular inquiry. Our only hope of finding Doctor Yen Sin, and getting Cyrus Greenwood's secret, was to bluff Locke. I even let him think I suspected you, tonight, in order to get his guard down."

"What is that secret?" interjected Dodd. "You said it was something for mass murder, but Locke kept you from finishing."

"I don't know all of it," Traile said soberly. "I found a clue in one of Cyrus Greenwood's books—Locke dropped it when he rushed out through that conduit. Greenwood had written part of a formula with invisible ink, right over the printing, but I finally brought it out. Also, I called Washington yesterday through the Q-Station, while Eric was out, and I secured information on Greenwood, along with some on Locke. Greenwood was a research engineer in nineteen eighteen, working in acoustics and beam transmission of sound. In nineteen thirty-four he developed a means of sending audible messages down an ordinary searchlight beam. The Navy experimented with it in connection with the Akron and the Macon. The sound couldn't be heard outside the beam."

"So that's how we heard Yen Sin's voice tonight!" exclaimed Dodd.

"Yes, Greenwood must also have devised some means for projecting an image down a visible beam. But, from the formula in that book, he must have gone on and developed a system of sending messages down invisible rays of ultraviolet light. There's nothing very mysterious about that, but it would be important for military and naval forces, as an enemy couldn't detect it easily."

Parker grazed a street-car and whirled south into Stockton Street.

"But where does the mass-murder idea come in?" he asked hurriedly.

"I'm not sure," muttered Traile. "I imagine Greenwood stumbled onto that part by accident—but whatever it is, his statement says that it kills at short range, and shrivels victims into a state resembling mummies, at a greater distance."

"Good Lord!" said Dodd in an awed tone. "Then that's what happened to Tanati and Greenwood's nephew!"

Traile grimly nodded.

"That's the answer. I think Cyrus Greenwood intended to have the Army give the thing a secret test. Major Locke, as an Intelligence officer, has a connection with the Corps Area Official Secrets Board. Greenwood probably approached him about the test. Locke saw a chance to steal the idea and sell it to some foreign power at a huge price. He kidnapped the old man and took the device. But Greenwood was cagey. He had left the formula, and some vital details on operating the device, noted down in six ordinary books, written in invisible ink, as I told you. He had arranged for his nephew to bring him the books, on pretext of finding him a job, if he found everything all right. Locke evidently saw it would be difficult to reproduce the apparatus, or else some foreign agent demanded the plans. So he forced Greenwood to tell him about the books, then sent a wire to Paul.

"But, meantime, Doctor Yen Sin had heard about the device through his spies—probably Tanati, for she posed as a foreign agent. And here's where his fiendish ability shows. He learned about the mummy effect, and knew that foreign agents would be fighting to buy the secret as soon as they were convinced of its possibilities. So he decided to make it look like a fake until he could get it into his hands."

"Then Meredith was working with him?" said Dodd, startled.

"No, he was an innocent victim," returned Traile. "The Doctor simply picked the easiest source to obtain a real mummy. Knowing him, I'm positive he kidnapped Meredith's daughter, and forced Meredith to keep it a secret and agree to the mummy trick, under threat of killing her. I suppose he used hypnotism

124

to make them forget the entire affair. His mental powers are incredible."

HE GAZED ahead, as they dashed past Jackson Street. "Turn left, when we reach Sacramento," he said to the Army captain. Parker nodded quickly, pressed down on the gas. Dodd stared across at Traile.

"How did you dope out the mummy trick?" he asked.

"I knew it was a fake almost at once," Traile answered. "But everything had happened so fast I was a little dazed. I could tell Meredith was in on the trick, and I had proof of it when I took that scarab. It had been glued there merely for effect—but it was an entirely different dynasty from the mummy-case."

"But if Tanati was Yen Sin's agent—" began Dodd. Then he looked horrified. "Good Heaven, you mean he deliberately sacrificed her?"

"Nothing else," said Traile. "It would mean little to him. His agents are simply pawns. That incident is an example of his deliberate, cold-blooded scheming. He didn't know who Monsieur X was, but he made some kind of contact with one of his agents, through Tanati. I suppose she pretended to be interested in buying the secret. Then Doctor Yen Sin learned that a demonstration was demanded by one or more foreign agents, probably Rudermann and the Japanese.

"He must have caused Tanati to be suspected by Monsieur X, possibly made him think she was a Government agent, so he would logically pick her as a good demonstration victim. No matter how Yen Sin worked it, it's certain he did it. He selected her, undoubtedly, because of her peculiar features—I shouldn't

125

be surprised to learn she had a trace of Egyptian blood. Her coiffure and dress accentuated the effect—another idea of the Doctor's, I suppose. He had her carry that cat—probably told her it was a signal to someone she was to meet. Perhaps she thought she was going to hear a test of Greenwood's 'directional signal' along the invisible light beam. But I think she suspected something was wrong—she had a frightened look just before it happened."

"God!" whispered the F.B.I. man. "I've met some cold-blooded gangsters, but this gives me the shivers."

"The Doctor is devoid of pity," Traile said in a grim voice. "He was even there to see that his scheme did not fail. Locke must not have trusted the foreign agents he was dealing with—they would be likely to seize the device if they knew where it was. That's the most probable reason for the thing being staged that way. He simply told them to be near there and see what happened. But Yen Sin had the mummy-case ready, with a mummified cat and a duplicate wrist-band and chain—tarnished to make an effect. He knew there'd be an interval, after it was over, before the others would risk getting in the 'beam', or whatever it is. And, in those few seconds, he switched in the mummy, and carried off Tanati.

"The only hitch was that she wasn't killed, and one of his men stabbed her when she struggled. That's why we found the bloody dagger in the mummy's breast—to carry out the illusion for anyone who had seen the murder. And the earlier tip to the police, which brought them within a block or so of that corner, was to insure that Meredith's 'mummy theft' story would be given plenty of publicity and build up the idea that Monsieur X was trying to hoax the foreign spies. That would hold up his deal long enough for Yen Sin to find him or the apparatus."

"Well, Yen Sin's got it now—that's certain," Dodd said huskily. "Lord! What if he spots us and turns it on?"

"We'd have a brief warning—the wailing sound," Traile muttered.

"I'll probably freeze in my tracks," said Dodd, "if it's the same thing we heard back there at your station."

TRAILE'S DARK eyes were watching the street. "It was the sound I heard just before Tanati was stricken—and later, from Paul Greenwood's lips after it had happened to him. There at the last, just before Tanati was stabbed, I think she was trying to sing that same queer song. Apparently the victims' brains are stunned so that they keep repeating what they heard last. It's the only explanation I can think of."

"Then you think they were turned into mummies by hearing that song?" said Dodd, aghast.

"Greenwood's formula—the part I have—hints at the wailing sound being a carrier beam for deadly vibrations," Traile answered. "That would explain why the cat died when Tanati was only stricken into that mummy state. Cats and other animals can hear sounds beyond the range of the human ear. I believe some high-pitched vibration first drove it mad and then stopped its heart."

The car swung into Sacramento Street. Captain Parker looked back for an instant, his shrewd young face pale with tension.

"This thing is more horrible than I dreamed! Think what

127

would happen if we were at war and some other country had that invention!"

Traile's bronzed face was somber.

"It couldn't be in more dangerous hands than it is," he said. "We'll have to strike fast, or he'll have it hidden where we'll never find it. Greenwood tried to say where it was, and we know it was on top of some pagoda-roofed building. There are scores of them in Chinatown, but we can narrow it down. It must be within a block of the spot where Locke disappeared last night."

"Then if we can follow him—" began Parker hastily.

"No! Yen Sin would be warned before we were halfway inside his base, if we followed Locke in force. Even if you and Dodd could get your reserves there in time, we'd find an empty nest. There's only one way to work it."

He explained rapidly, as the Army car sped down Sacramento Street.

"But it's plain suicide—your part!" exclaimed Dodd.

"Not if I work it right," said Traile. "And I can't let Eric fall into that yellow devil's hands!"

He directed Parker to turn as they neared the next alley.

"I'll drop off," he said quickly. "Drive through to Clay Street—fast! Then follow the plan!"

"Let me go with you," pleaded Dodd. "The captain can take charge."

Traile dropped his hand on Dodd's shoulder.

"Thanks, old chap—but this way's best."

He was out on the running-board, the moment the car plunged into the dark alley. With a last admonition for speed, he jumped. The car raced away, and he was left alone. He ran noiselessly to a cross-alley sixty feet away. In a few seconds, he was in the narrow passage from which Sonya had come to warn him and Eric, two nights ago. He shot a glance toward the street, then turned to the right, squeezing between two buildings which almost touched each other.

He emerged in a black, foul-smelling courtyard. It was here that he had lost Locke on the previous night. No alley led into the place. It seemed to have been designed for dark and evil purposes. He felt inside his coat for his .38, then slowly withdrew his hand.

The shoulder harness was empty.

He remembered at once how he had tumbled into the Army car, and the jerk of Parker's hasty start. The gun must have fallen to the floor at that moment. But it was small comfort to know how he had lost it. He groped in his coat, found his pocket-knife. It might be of use in a pinch.

Silently, he crept through the courtyard, feeling his way along the walls, pausing to listen when he found a door. He could hear nothing save a subdued bustle from Grant Avenue. Then minutes passed. With growing despair, he began to fear that Locke had already arrived or entered the base from another point.

All the doors he had found were heavily barred. He gazed up, looking for the curling eaves of a pagoda roof against the vague light from adjacent streets. There was one temple-shaped roof, but two other structures towered above it. He waited another minute, then turned back hopelessly. The only chance now was to join Parker and Dodd, and he knew by the time his plan was carried out that Eric's fate would surely be sealed. Perhaps, even now....

He wheeled, staring up from the entry of the narrow passage. A jagged patch of light showed high above him, and he heard a tinkling as glass fell to the courtyard. Suddenly, a man appeared in the light, his fists beating frenziedly at the broken black glass which remained. From somewhere behind him came the angry squeal of an Oriental. The man half turned, still pounding at the heavy glass, and Traile saw his face clearly.

It was Cyrus Greenwood.

CHAPTER 12
THE ROOM OF THE LANTERNS

WITH A frenzy of desperation, the old man swung his legs through the broken window and dropped to the cornice beneath. A murderous yellow face appeared above him, just as he fell. A long, curved blade smashed the remaining glass from the window, then the Chinese sprang through the opening. His pigtail, hanging from under a black skullcap, writhed like a snake as he let himself drop.

Cyrus Greenwood had stumbled along the ledge, trying to reach a spot from which he could jump to another building. Just as he crouched for the leap, the assassin caught up. Traile groaned as he saw the curved blade whirl down. The old man threw one hand before him, toppled from the ledge. He struck on a slanting roof thirty feet below, rolled off and fell to the ground.

The pigtailed Chinese sprang across to the other building, let himself slide to the eaves. Holding his weapon in one hand, he lowered himself to another projecting ledge. He was about to drop the last few feet to the ground, when another Oriental cried shrilly from the broken window.

"Ai! The old one has escaped!"

"Quiet your stupid tongue!" snarled the pigtailed Chinese. "The Master may kill us both, if he learns of this."

"But if the old one reaches the police—"

"He is dead—or dying!" said the other man harshly. He dropped, cat-like, to the dark courtyard. "Turn out the light to hide the broken window," he added fiercely. "Then steal down and help me carry him inside before anyone finds he escaped."

The Chinese at the window disappeared. Traile had run forward in the shadows, was almost beside the crumpled figure there in the gloom. He jumped back as the pigtailed Oriental ran toward the dying man. Just before the light from the window went out, the yellow killer saw him. His breath whistled through his teeth in a startled hiss. Then he lifted the curved blade for a swift blow.

Traile threw himself flat, shot out his right foot. Kicked squarely on the kneecap, the Chinese sprawled over him with a howl of pain. Traile swiftly rolled over, crashed his fist behind the assassin's ear. The Chinese had jerked his head from the ground. It thudded back with a crunch, and the breath went out of him in a long sigh.

Old Cyrus Greenwood lay feebly moaning on the bricks a few yards away. As Traile knelt beside him, the old man gave a choked cry.

"Don't be afraid," Traile said gently. "I'm not one of Yen Sin's men."

He tried to lift the old man in his arms, but Greenwood groaned in anguish, and he felt warm blood on his hands.

"Put me down. It's too late now—" Greenwood's voice thickened, then Traile felt his broken body tense with sudden purpose. "Lean over," he said hoarsely. "Must warn country—before I'm finished—"

Traile bent, pityingly, as the brave old man drove himself to speak.

"Doctor Yen Sin—has invention I built—Army," Greenwood moaned. "Tried—force me to—"

"I know most of it," Traile said with a gentle swiftness. "I was in that room tonight, and I was with your nephew when Locke turned it on him."

"That monster!" groaned the dying man. "I saw it—turned it on Paul—afraid you would learn truth. But the Chinese—they stole machine from him—going to take it somewhere—build large ones."

"Where is it now?" Traile asked hurriedly, as Greenwood's voice faded away.

"Up—in tower," the old man whispered. "Think it is—Grant Avenue. But you can't—get up there. They'd turn it on you—kills at close range—sends terrific vibrations down audible sound track. It causes spasm in arteries—stops the heart—"

Traile looked around anxiously. "But tell me how to get into the—"

"God forgive me," the dying man mumbled. "I never meant—this. Trying—find secret signal beam—"

He seemed about to lapse into unconsciousness. Traile desperately shook his shoulder.

"Try to tell me how to get into the base!" he whispered.

The old man's pale, bruised face turned toward him. He made a final effort.

"Arched door—steps behind curtain," he said in a bare whisper. "Up—lantern room—pull third one to—"

Traile leaned closer.

"But where is the arched door?" he asked hastily. There was no answer, not even a last groan from that brave and broken figure. Gently, he lowered the old inventor's head and stood up. It was a moment before he could overcome the effect of Greenwood's death and force himself to the feverish thought required. There were two ways. He could wait and capture the other Chinese or—

QUICKLY, HE stooped over the man who had tried to kill him. The Oriental was alive, but his labored breathing gave evidence that he would probably never recover his senses. Traile rolled him out of his loose pajama-like coat, put it on over his own. He was fastening the silken knots when he heard the sound of a door being opened.

He dragged the unconscious Chinese to the passage entry, whipped out his knife and cut off the man's pigtail close to his head. Seizing the black skullcap, he held the pigtail on top of

Doctor Yen Sin tilted the machine,
to turn them into mummies.

his head and forced the cap firmly over it to hold it in place. As he ran back, he smeared his bloody hand across his face to hide his Caucasian features. Greenwood's blood. The old inventor still served, even in death.

The other Oriental was padding toward him in the darkness.

134

He spoke harshly, in the dialect the pigtailed man had used.

"What kept you? A tortoise could have moved faster!"

"I had to come through the second basement," said the other man nervously. "Something has happened. There is a new prisoner, and the Master himself was there."

Traile's heart turned cold. A prisoner? It was undoubtedly Eric.

"Take the American's shoulders," he ordered. "We must get him inside."

"Is he dead?" asked the nervous Chinese.

"Yes," said Traile gruffly. He tucked the sword under his arm, took the dead man's feet. "Go on—there is no time to be lost."

They moved toward the door, Traile maneuvering so that the other man led the way. He heard the anxious voice of a second Chinese as they entered a dark hall.

"Did you leave any signs?" the man asked.

"Only a little blood," Traile grunted. "In the dirt it will not show."

The door grated shut, and he heard bars sliding into their sockets. A moment later, a switch clicked and pale light shone in the hall. Traile kept his head down, silently praying that the difference in trousers would escape the door-guard's notice. The man helping him trotted along, and then soon went around a turn in the hallway. Traile breathed a little more freely.

The Chinese halted, jabbered briefly, and a cleverly concealed door swung open on the left. Another guard stood at this point. After a stare at the dead inventor, his slanting eyes lifted to Traile's blood-smeared face.

"*Shen mo szi?*" he exclaimed, letting the door close and lock. "What is the matter?"

"It is only blood from where I fell on this old man," Traile grunted. He tried to push by the Chinese, but the sword under his arm slipped and started to fall. As he caught it, the guard jumped toward him.

"*Ni kan!*" he howled at the other Oriental. "This man is a spy!"

His clutching fingers tore the pigtail loose, and the black skullcap fell to the floor. As the guard drew his gun, Traile leaped back, whirled the sword. The razor-like blade cut down through the yellow man's head as though it had been cardboard. As he slumped, the other man dropped his hold on the corpse and wildly ran ahead. Traile hurled the weapon after him. It twisted in mid-air, but the hilt struck the fleeing Chinese a glancing blow on the neck.

With a squeal of mortal terror, he collapsed to the floor. Then, as he realized his throat had not been cut, he snatched at the weapon. Traile dived like a football tackle. His plunge drove the man's breath from his lungs. He drove in a fierce left hook, crossed a hard right to the jaw. The Chinese slid back like a sack of wet grain, lay there with his mouth wide open.

TRAILE HAD to drag himself to his feet. Until that moment, he had not realized how long he had gone without relaxing his body. With a sick dismay, he knew he was near his limit. Unless he stopped for a vital recharging of strength, he might collapse from exhaustion. But there was no time to stop.

He leaned against the wall for a second, straining his ears for the sound of an alarm. He thought he could hear faint steps from the way they had come. But the second door was locked, and there would be a delay in the discovery that something was wrong. He picked up the dead guard's pistol, and moved doggedly ahead. The weariness grew upon him, and he knew he had but a few more minutes of action.

He came to a circular staircase, which led up into gloom. There seemed no other way. He began to climb, gripping the handrail, grimly forcing himself on. The thought of Eric's peril gave him a brief burst of strength. His lagging steps quickened, but when he reached the top his brow was dripping with perspiration. He took off the Chinese coat and wiped his wet and bloody face. It made small difference now. In ordinary light, anyone could see he was not Chinese.

With a tingling of weary pulses, he saw an arched door nearby. He gazed around, glimpsed a set of dark portières. He parted them and saw another flight of stairs. There were only seven steps, but his heart was pounding as he came to the last one.

"Lantern room," he muttered. "Must be—through here."

There were two ebony doors, but they were partly opened. He thought he heard someone moving around beyond them. Holding to the edge of one door, he peered inside. It appeared to be a small conference-room, but there was no one in sight. A large temple lamp was suspended from the center of the ceiling, with several small, decorated lanterns equally spaced about it.

A muffled cry from somewhere, so faint he could not tell if it came from a man or a woman, brought his taut nerves to an edge. He stumbled forward, pulled the copper chain of the nearest lantern. There was no result. He jerked the next, and the next. No time now to puzzle out which one poor old Greenwood meant.

The fourth chain resisted his tug. He pulled harder. A section of the ebony wall pivoted silently and he saw an open space beyond. He staggered through, found himself in a strange room.

The faint light failed to bring out the color in the tapestries, made them seem as dark and somber as the ceiling. On a large rectangular table was a miniature City of San Francisco, amazingly correct in detail. Colored lights shone in some of the tiny buildings, and he saw that there was a row of buttons recessed near one end of the table, before a large, carved chair.

It came to him then that he had found the nerve center of Doctor Yen Sin's base. The miniature city was evidently part of the Crime Emperor's secret-communication system, built so that he could tell at a glance the exact position of any spy who was reporting.

But of the Yellow Doctor himself there was no sign.

TRAILE STUMBLED against the table, looked feverishly around the room. There was apparently no other exit, yet he knew there must be one. Yen Sin would have at least two escapes from this important spot. He felt along the walls, but his hasty tapping was deadened by the thick tapestries, and he could find no place which sounded hollow.

He was about to give up, and retrace his way through the lantern room, when again he heard a cry. This time it was a man's voice, raised in fierce emotion. The blood suddenly leaped through his veins as he recognized it for Eric. He spun around to the miniature city, bent over the row of buttons. One of them might control another secret exit. He jabbed at the first on the right. A blue light glowed in a tiny office building.

"Acting control, Group Three," a voice spoke promptly.

Traile started. The words seemed to have come from the solid wall. Then he realized the answer. He pressed the second button, saw a green light glow, raked his hand over all the remaining buttons. A spotlight went on at the end of the room, and curtains drew back, exposing a glass-fronted cell. He started toward it, ignoring the clamor of voices from the hidden amplifier. The din ended abruptly, as though a main switch had been thrown at some other receiving point. Then he heard Sonya Damitri cry out wildly.

"Anything but that! Have pity on him!"

A tapestry-covered door had opened on the right. It was through this that her voice was coming. Traile staggered to the opening, his aching muscles gripping the automatic. Then, with absolute horror, he glimpsed the scene before him.

In the center of a dungeon-like room was a queer-looking apparatus like a searchlight, mounted on coils and black transformers. Tubes were glowing brightly on one side, and he, in his hasty glance, saw a small microphone above a lens, like a television scanning-glass. At the rear of another bank of coils was a switchboard, and, back of this, one yellow claw on a rheostat, was Doctor Yen Sin.

All this he saw in a fraction of a second, then his sickened eyes flashed past the apparatus. At one side, barely out of range, stood Sonya Damitri. Her hands were bound behind her back and her exotically beautiful face was white with an awful fear. Chained to the wall, near her, was a mummified figure, stripped to the waist.

And, manacled beside him, directly in front of that deadly machine, was Eric Gordon!

CHAPTER 13
THE PAGODA-TOP OF YEN SIN

IN THAT first terrible moment, Traile stood paralyzed in the secret doorway. A hoarse voice brought him out of his daze. "Kill!" it croaked. "Kill! Kill!"

The words came from the drooling lips of the mummy-man, as he lunged against his chains. And, then with a final horror, Traile saw that it was Paul Greenwood. The Yellow Doctor's malignant face turned toward the drooling figure, then he looked back at Eric.

"An excellent idea," he said mockingly, "but too swift an end. And I do not wish to rob Sonya of her charming lover, merely to alter that charm slightly."

Eric's tortured blue eyes never left Sonya's face.

"Goodbye," he whispered. "Don't pity me—afterward. Pretend it's—"

The rasp of a low-pitched buzzer sounded straight back of Traile. He jumped from the doorway, forcing his fast-waning strength into one last, quick action. Astonishment raced over Sonya's pale face, as he sprang toward the Yellow Doctor. Yen Sin whirled, then stark rage came into his tawny eyes.

"*Hwan ban!* Guards!" he cried in a voice of rising fury.

Traile drove the gun hard against him, and his words ended in a gasp. With another jab, Traile drove the Crime Emperor away from the machine, then gave it a quick shove. It swung around on its rollers, so that the sinister projector no longer pointed at Eric.

"Thank God!" Sonya said in a broken voice.

Traile moved sidewise, reaching out toward Eric's shackles. For the instant his weariness was gone and a fierce exhilaration swept over him. He jerked the iron pin from Eric's right hand-cuff, and the hinged manacle flew open. The torture died out of the younger man's face. He tried to speak, but his lips only moved convulsively.

"Quick, old man!" Traile muttered. "Unfasten the other one. I'm on the edge of—"

141

The Yellow Doctor's eyes slitted sharply as he saw Traile sway. But Traile recovered himself. Eric frantically released his left hand, wheeled around to Sonya.

"No, no!" she said wildly. "Escape while you can!"

"And leave you to be tortured?" cried Eric. He unfastened her bonds, pulled them away with desperate haste.

The buzzer in the room with the tiny city gave a prolonged signal. Traile held onto the ray-machine, twitched a glance toward the chamber. He saw no one there, but in the shadows of the room where he stood, a heavy door had opened. He flung a hoarse warning at Eric and Sonya.

For there, in the entry, was a glaring Malay with a blowgun at his lips!

Traile swayed back, raised his gun in leaden fingers. With a vicious hiss, a feathered dart shot from the hollow tube. Traile slumped to his knees, and the dart struck the ray-machine. He heard Sonya scream, caught a flash of yellow mandarin robes. He tried to swivel around—

Then the gun was torn from his nerveless hand, and he toppled to the floor.

As through a haze, he saw the mocking face of Yen Sin looking over the gun… saw a sudden rush of Malays and Chinese, and Eric and Sonya seized… felt a brutal kick, and recognized the hulking Pole he had wounded two nights before.

He could see, hear and feel—but he lay there helpless. In that brief moment of exhilaration, in capturing Yen Sin, he had used the last bit of energy his sleepless body had stored.

"Again!" he heard the Crime Emperor's voice. The giant Pole

kicked him fiercely in the ribs. Then Doctor Yen Sin nodded. "Enough—he is not pretending."

He turned, and Traile saw the Chinese he had knocked out and left in the basement. The man's jaw was swollen, and he wobbled as two other Orientals brought him in. He told, in a frightened voice, what had occurred. Traile lay as though in a stupor, while Yen Sin questioned the man. This was his last chance… if he could recharge his overtaxed nerves and muscles with sufficient energy, before Yen Sin suspected….

"Are you sure," he heard the Yellow Doctor ask, "that no one else was with him?"

"Yes, Master, I am certain," the frightened Chinese answered. "And Fo Leng, the first-door guard, says he also is sure—"

"For attempting to deceive me," said Yen Sin, "thirty lashes and an hour on the rack." He motioned for the guards to take away the cowering wretch, then looked down at the helpless Q-Man.

"So you failed to carry a supply of the drug with you this time, Mr. Traile?"

TRAILE MADE no answer. He could feel a slow building up of energy, but his nerves were like taut wires. Paul Greenwood croaked: "Kill! Kill!" He tugged at his chains, glaring insanely about the room.

Doctor Yen Sin glanced at him with annoyance. The burly Pole made a meaning gesture with his huge hands. "If you wish him silent, Master—"

"Not yet," said the Crime Emperor. "I wish to study him further. And he must not die violently. It is important that it

143

be as quiet as possible, so my autopsy will be accurate. There is much we do not know about the effect of this device."

"But I thought," said the other man apologetically, "that the Army officer explained—"

Yen Sin's weird eyes took on a contemptuous light.

"He is a fool. He knows only that commands sent down the beam, after a victim is already stunned, are sometimes obeyed. I intend to find why the command takes permanent possession of the victim's brain, as with this mumbling fool here."

Traile's eyes shifted briefly to the ray-machine. He thought he was unobserved, but Doctor Yen Sin smiled sardonically.

"Perhaps, I can satisfy your curiosity, my dear Traile. I might even give you a—personal demonstration."

Eric Gordon groaned. The Crime Emperor looked at him, then ordered the huge Polish agent to lift Traile to his feet. The man did it with a venomous jerk, gripped Traile's arm with massive fingers. But in spite of the pain, Traile felt a brief elation. The haze had cleared. His brain was beginning to work again.

"Search him," directed the Yellow Doctor. "He may have been carrying additional weapons."

A wiry little Chinese made the search, while the Pole held Traile. The Oriental felt the lining of Traile's coat, expertly slit it open.

"Here is something he was hiding, Master."

Traile's heart sank. He had hoped they would not find the decoded pages from Cyrus Greenwood's book. In the excitement of pursuing Locke, he had forgotten the pages were sewed in his coat.

Doctor Yen Sin glanced quickly over the sheets, then an unholy triumph blazed in his tawny eyes.

"The missing part of the formula! I shall soon fit it with the rest and understand the entire secret. Pray accept my thanks, Mr. Traile. Because of Locke's bungling, I was afraid I would have to rely on my own technical knowledge, in building larger machines from this small one, and there were certain points which troubled me. Cyrus Greenwood was a genius."

Traile did not reply. The gloating Chinese continued.

"Perhaps, in a few years, your country may learn a little more about the mummy-death. These plans make it possible to build machines of enough power to reach high-flying aircraft and kill the pilots. After Japan's armies and air force have been subdued, I may be able to unite the East. Perhaps your haughty white race may have a surprise and a Chinese master!"

Traile heard a quickly stifled exclamation at the Yellow Doctor's last words. From the corner of his eye he saw Iris Vaughan. The blond English girl had evidently just entered. Yen Sin nodded mockingly as he saw her.

"You might ask this pretty child, Mr. Traile, how she likes to serve a yellow master."

A slow flush dyed the girl's face. Her luminous blue eyes met Traile's for an instant, then she quickly looked away. In spite of all she had done, Traile felt a surge of pity for her. She seemed the victim of a dual personality—one perhaps purposely developed by Yen Sin through the studied use of opium.

"But we waste time," said the Crime Emperor, with a subtle

hardening of tone, "Now that I have these plans, I have but one interest in you, Mr. Traile. You know to what I refer."

TRAILE DID not speak. His gaze went to the drooling mummy-man, and he watched as the stricken creature pulled and tore at his chains. Yen Sin continued after a brief pause.

"Owing to my recent unfortunate retreat from New York, my detailed reports on you are incomplete. But I have proof that on at least one occasion you have gone without sleep for a period of five days and thirteen hours. I am aware that you have traveled in all parts of the world, and it is obvious you have found some peculiar drug in an out-of-the-way spot, which you are using to accomplish this purpose."

Traile stood, dull-eyed, relaxing as much as possible in his standing position. His heart was steady again. The weariness was gone from his muscles. If he could trick them long enough to get at the machine....

"I shall give you your choice," the Yellow Doctor said in a silky voice. "Give me the secret, and you may have the option of joining the Empire—or a quick death. Refuse—and you will slowly, very slowly, become a living mummy."

Though he had known that some frightful torture was in store for him, Traile turned cold with horror.

"Perhaps three or four days, perhaps a week," Yen Sin went on smoothly. "It will be an interesting experiment—"

"You damned fiend!" moaned Eric Gordon.

"—As compared with the swifter effect on your reckless comrade," said the Crime Emperor. "What is your answer, Mr. Traile?"

Traile's eyes were lowered with a hopeless look. He had measured the distance to the machine. Three swift moves—

"Master!" shouted a frenzied voice. A stocky Chinese in American clothes plunged into the room. "The ray-machine! We must get it up to the roof or we are lost!"

Traile groaned. Three men had leaped to the apparatus. His chance was gone.

"What has happened?" Yen Sin demanded swiftly.

"We have been tricked!" cried the stocky Chinese. He pointed fiercely, and Traile saw Locke cringing near the Oriental. "He said they had shaken off all pursuit—but soldiers with machine guns are on the roofs all about us!"

"I swear we weren't followed!" Locke burst out, as Yen Sin's gaze fell on him. "They must have found out some other way."

"Traile!" said the Yellow Doctor. He turned with a deadly calmness. "Chain him to the wall. I'll deal with him later. The rest of you move the machine."

His men swarmed about the ray-machine. The heavy power cable was disconnected, and the device was rolled hastily to the door where the first Malay had entered. The huge Polish agent shoved Traile back against the wall, and one of the Chinese fastened the right-hand manacle. The Yellow Doctor turned with a sharp command.

"Kerokowski! Hurry to the roof—Ho Lun and his men can handle Traile now."

As the giant dashed off, the Crime Emperor beckoned imperiously to Iris Vaughan.

"Go down to Second Control. Order them to stand by for

immediate transfer. Also, have them double the guard on all exits."

The blond girl nodded fearfully, disappeared through the room containing the miniature city. Doctor Yen Sin turned back to Traile with a look of icily controlled hate.

"I shall return after I dispose of your soldiers. This will probably force me to transfer to another base—but I think you will regret having been the cause."

He stalked out, his yellow robes swishing about him.

"Kill!" muttered the pitiful creature fastened to the wall. He rattled his chains and snarled at Ho Lun, the plump Chinese left in charge.

HO LUN swore at him, the thug keeping Traile covered with his gun while another Oriental reached for the left-hand manacle. Traile had caught Eric's eye, where the younger man stood with Sonya, guarded by two armed men. But there was only a puzzled, helpless look on Eric's face in response to his furtive signal.

As Ho Lun's assistant started to close the hinged handcuff about Traile's left arm, Traile let himself sag down limply. The Chinese gave him a stinging slap. Traile pretended to stumble, kicked against Paul Greenwood. The stricken boy jumped angrily, gave a furious snarl. Traile darted a look at the mummy-man's left handcuff as the Chinese pulled him to his feet. He had already noted that the pin had gradually worked up during Greenwood's restless struggles. One more jerk, and it would come out. If he could only free the other....

He raised his left hand, with an air of hopeless submission.

The Chinese again seized the handcuff, started to fasten it. With a violent lunge, Traile shot his free hand across and snatched the pin from Greenwood's right manacle.

Ho Lun gave a screech and leaped to seize the iron cuff before it could open. But his leap was not fast enough, and the manacle flew open. The mummy-man lurched forward, and, with a snap, the other handcuff pin came out. The other Chinese had struck fiercely at Traile.

The tall American whipped his hand down at the yellow man's neck. Its stiffened edge struck like a solid bar. With a strangled sound, the Chinese tottered into Paul Greenwood's path.

"Kill!" cried the mummy-man hoarsely. His hideous hands closed on the other man's throat. Already stunned, the ill-fated Oriental tumbled down in a heap. Ho Lun had sprung backward, his slant eyes bulging in terror. The mummy-man lurched across the Chinese he had dropped, groped at Ho Lun.

Traile hurriedly unfastened the right handcuff with his left hand.

"Michael!" came Eric's hasty voice. "Look out—the man on your right!"

Traile spun around. One of the other two guards had run to help Ho Lun. The Chinese was aiming his gun at Paul Greenwood, but, as Traile whirled, he hastily swerved the weapon. Traile dived at the man's legs. The pistol blasted above his head, then abruptly a second shot rang out, and the Oriental tumbled down upon him.

He threw off the limp body, snatched the gun and jumped

149

up. Twenty feet away, Eric stood with a smoking pistol. The guard, from whom he had seized it, was doubled up on the floor, both hands holding his middle.

Traile heard a half-choked scream, saw Ho Lun in the grip of Paul Greenwood. The Chinese crashed back against a screen, and, for a moment, was free. As the mummy-man lunged at him again, Ho Lun fired blindly. Paul Greenwood's shriveled face twisted in animal fury. With a clumsy, bear-like spring, he threw himself on Ho Lun. The gun roared again, and, with a whimpering cry, the mummy-man collapsed.

But his terrible hands were closed tight on the throat of Ho Lun.

SOMEONE CAUGHT at Traile's arm, and he turned to see Eric's tense face. Back of him was Sonya, her great black eyes wide with horror. "Quickly—this way!" she gasped. "I'll try to get you out!"

"Go with her, Eric!" said Traile. He raced for the opposite doorway.

"Eric—you'll be killed!" he suddenly heard Sonya cry. Then the younger man was back at his side, a crooked grin on his lips.

"I'm with you, Michael! Let's go!"

"It can't be far to the roof," Traile muttered. "There's an elevator shaft—they probably took the thing up that way."

In a second, they found the stairs and dashed upward. Eric shot a look back, as they came to the first landing.

"Sonya!" he shouted desperately. "For Heaven's sake—go back!"

A sudden droning sound above them drowned her answer. "Good God!" cried Eric. "They're turning it on the soldiers!" "No, not yet!" rasped Traile. "That's one of the—"

Crack! A gun roared from above them, and he saw the distorted face of the Polish agent. The bullet clanged against one side of the small elevator shaft. Traile pumped a quick shot upward, just as the man aimed again. The giant rose up as though for a queer dance-step. Then he tipped forward and came hurtling down the steps.

Traile jumped to the side and dashed on up, with Eric close behind. The droning sound had increased, was now recognizable as the roar of an airplane motor. But for this, the shots would certainly have been heard upon the roof. The last flight of steps was shrouded in gloom, but Traile could see the outlines of a fairly large trapdoor.

They were almost at the top when a dazzling light blazed up in the sky over Chinatown. Traile leaped up through the trap. A parachute flare was slowly swinging down, casting its brilliant glare for hundreds of yards around. Silhouetted in the light were five or six of Yen Sin's men.

Ten feet away stood the deadly ray-machine, its heavy power cable plugged into the elevator platform on which it rested. Back of the machine was the Yellow Doctor.

A freezing sensation came over Traile as he saw where the thing was pointed. Between several curling pagoda roofs were ordinary roofs, all of them brightly visible. On three of the flat roofs, he could see squads of soldiers and agents.

And Doctor Yen Sin was tilting the machine to turn them into mummies!

Traile leveled his gun, but a man suddenly sprang from the shadows. He fired, and the killer went down. Yen Sin whirled, and his furious eyes swept over Traile. Then he was hidden by the rush of assassins to down the American.

Traile's gun was knocked from his hand. He lashed out at the nearest face, saw it twist with pain. A Chinese gunman leaped across the platform, but, in the wild struggle, his shot went up through the roof. By now the drone of the unseen plane had grown to a deafening bellow. Abruptly, an Army ship dived underneath the flare.

A PISTOL flamed at Traile's left, and a man beside him dropped. He saw Eric with a gun, and over Eric's shoulder the stark-white face of lovely Sonya Damitri. A clawing assassin jumped on Traile's back. Traile threw him off, sprang toward the ray-machine. Doctor Yen Sin had swiveled it around, was aiming it toward the plane. Traile clutched at the aiming-wheel, gave it a violent spin. The deadly searchlight swung in the other direction.

As it moved, a man leaped wildly away from one corner. Until that second, Traile had thought his crouching figure part of the huge gargoyle which supported that end of the roof. Then the light of the drifting flare fell on his fear-stricken features, and he saw it was Major Locke.

The Army plane roared close by, banked in a hasty turn. Another flare turned the night into day. Doctor Yen Sin seized a rheostat handle. Traile lunged at the apparatus, two men trying to drag him down. They struck the side of the ray-machine, and it slid back on its wheels. One man jumped madly to catch it—and in that instant Yen Sin threw the rheostat.

A frightful, wailing sound burst from the ray-machine. Half-stunned, Traile saw two Chinese stagger back to the edge of the roof. An icy shudder ran down his spine. Caught by the full force of the invisible beam, they had been instantly mummified!

Crazed with terror, Locke dashed for the trap in the floor. As he neared it, he tried to hurl Sonya out of his way. But his flailing hands had barely touched her when Eric leaped to the rescue. The Southerner's fist crashed fiercely into the major's face. Already off balance, the terrified spy plunged backward into the beam.

As if by some dreadful magic, he shriveled, grew aged in an instant. He rolled to the edge of the roof, and, for one awful moment, his hideous, darkened face glared up at the gargoyle above him. Then his weakly clutching fingers lost their hold and he disappeared from view.

A shrieking Chinese ran past Traile, all thought of murder abandoned. Back of the trembling ray-machine Yen Sin still was crouching, his face like some devilish mask. Traile started toward him, stumbled over the man whom Eric had shot.

The deadly searchlight whirled around at him as he fell. Desperately, he seized the power cable and pulled it from the socket. There was a final, ear-splitting howl—and the ray-machine went dead.

Into the face of Doctor Yen Sin came a dazed and beaten

look. He stepped back helplessly as Traile regained his feet. Then, with a dexterous twist, he sent the silenced machine rolling into Traile's path. Before Traile could shove it out of his way, Yen Sin was across at the other side of the roof. A section of one carved-and-gilded gargoyle opened at his touch. He sprang inside—and was gone.

Traile ran to the spot, stared down into the hollow column. Only darkness showed inside. He glanced quickly across to the roof of the nearest building. By the glow of the second flare, he could see a group of men, some in uniform. They were signaling, and, in a moment, he recognized Dodd and Parker. He shouted across the intervening space, saw them hurry down, surround and raid the base. As he turned back, he saw Sonya there with Eric.

"They will never catch him," she said. She pointed to the gargoyle. "It leads to a spiral escape tube, with hidden openings on every floor and down in the secret basements."

TRAILE BENT over, picked up a tangle of yellow silk. It was obviously a pocket which had caught on a claw of the gargoyle. As he pulled it loose, some torn and crumpled paper fell to the floor. The grimness left his deep-tanned face.

"Yes," he said calmly, "the Doctor has escaped. But his dream of a super ray-machine will have to remain a dream. Without these sheets he will be helpless."

"I am glad," the girl said simply. She looked at Eric, and Traile glanced away as he saw what was in their eyes.

Minutes later, when the Army squads and the F.B.I. men

could be heard coming up through the building, he turned and smiled at them.

"Go down to the landing, you two, and wait for me a minute. I've something to do before those others come."

He watched them, a trifle sadly, as they started down the stairs. The shadow of danger would always be dark about them. The Yellow Doctor would never forget nor forgive. But for a little time, they might find happiness. Perhaps, he could keep them guarded....

He wheeled back to the ray-machine. A few blows with the butt of a gun, that and the wires jerked loose. The Army would be displeased—but it was better this way. He raised the gun, paused, then slowly nodded. Brave old Cyrus Greenwood would have wanted it this way.

POPULAR PUBLICATIONS
HERO PULPS

LOOK FOR MORE SOON!

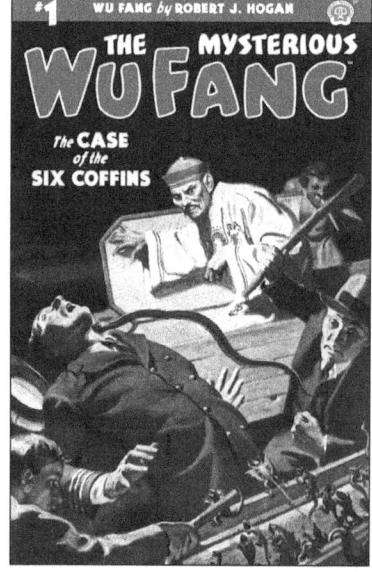